THE TWISTED TREE TRIANGLE

BY

SUSAN L. PARÉ

Printed in the United States of America.
First Edition: 2021.2
All rights reserved.
Cover designed by Susan L. Paré
Cover picture – Seattle Magazine
ISBN-13: 978-1-7335572-7-6

MORE BY THIS AUTHOR

The Box House

The Proof Is In the Pudding

Blueberries and Bears and My Brother's Shoes

Red, White, and Blue (A Short Story)

She Never Stopped Talking

Red

The House on Ludington Street

What's Behind the Screen Door?

The Mayor's Son

Willerton Woods

Cowtown

Floating Face Down
A Sheriff "Cowboy" Berkson Mystery Novel – Book Three

Let's Play Autopsy

A Bad Week In Hollister
A Sheriff "Cowboy" Berkson Mystery Novel – Book Two

Don't Smother Your Mother
A Sheriff "Cowboy" Berkson Mystery Novel – Book One

Crossing Sydney

Index

THE TWISTED TREE TRIANGLE

THE TWISTED TREE TRIANGLE   Susan L. Paré

Chapter One

"We'll take it," Jack Keegan told the realtor.

Janice Harper wanted to throw her arms around the man and hug him. This was her biggest sale ever and she could hear the beaches in Hawaii calling to her to come and play in the sand. "That's wonderful," she said, hoping her voice wasn't giving away her excitement. "What kind of an offer do you plan to make?"

"I'll pay full price if he throws in the furniture. I like what he's done and my wife isn't much of a decorator. If he leaves it all, you can tell him it's a done deal."

"I'll call him right now and let him know you're interested and see what he says about the furnishings."

"You do that. I'm going to check the outside again."

Janice watched as Keegan walked to the front door. Her legs were trembling so badly, she thought she would fall to the floor. She plunked herself down in a chair and pulled out her phone, laughing when she noticed how badly her hands were shaking. She was the listing agent for this property and finding a buyer meant that she didn't have to share the commission. She punched in the seller's number and waited. "Mr. Sinclair, Janice Harper here. I've got a buyer for the lake property. There's just one thing we need to discuss, though."

Jack Keegan walked over to his wife, Maggie, and smiled. "I told her yes," he told her.

Maggie smiled back at him. "I'm glad. I think the boys are going to love it here."

"Do you really think so?" Jack asked her. "I don't think they are going to like the idea of leaving all their friends behind."

"They can make new friends, Jack. My God, how many kids can grow up in an environment like this? A home big enough to get lost in with their own swimming pool, a lake in the back yard where they can go boating and fishing, and ..."

"I get it," Jack interrupted. "But we're still dragging them out of the city into a totally foreign environment. I think it's gonna be hard on them."

"Perhaps," Maggie said. "But, they're young enough to adjust. Did you ask Janice if the neighbors had any kids?"

"You mean that house down the road from here?"

"It's the only other house around here, isn't it?"

"I guess. It is pretty secluded out here. And, no, I haven't asked her about the neighbors." Jack turned as he saw Janice walking towards them.

"Good news," she told the couple. "Except for a few pieces of furniture, Mr. Sinclair has agreed to leave the rest. There are a few pieces that have been in his family for years and he will be taking those with him."

Maggie smiled. "That's wonderful. It looks like we bought ourselves a new home, Jack."

Jack shook his head, agreeing with her. "It sure does. Let's go draw up those papers, shall we, Janice?"

"Let me be the first to congratulate you," Janice said, smiling. "I know you're going to love it here."

"I'm certain we will. I just hope the boys will feel the same way."

"It will probably be a big adjustment for them, coming from a big city and all. Fortunately, the schools here are excellent, and the town is big on sports. This is a great area to live in. How old are your boys?"

"Michael is fourteen and Alex will be twelve next month."

"So, I guess it won't be long before Michael will be driving."

"Dear God, don't remind me," Maggie replied. "I dread it already."

"It will be fine, Maggie," Jack said. "By the way, we were wondering if the neighbors down the road have any kids."

"Sullivan is their name. Fred and Lucy Sullivan. They do but their children are all grown and living elsewhere. Fred and Lucy usually go south in the winter. I'm afraid there are no other families around here with kids. However, school will be starting before long and I'm sure Michael and Alex will make lots of new friends.

"Did you want to look around anymore, Jack?" Maggie asked. "It's getting late and I'm sure Janice would like to go back to the office and start the paperwork."

"I'm fine. Let's go."

"If you don't mind my asking, Jack, what do you do for a living?"

"I'm unemployed at the moment," he replied smiling. "I was a maintenance engineer before I quit my job."

Maggie laughed. "That's just a fancy title for a janitor," she said. "Jack worked at the high school before he retired."

"I see," Janice said, looking concerned. "Do you work, Maggie?"

"Not anymore," Maggie said smiling. "We're both retired. Right, Jack?"

"That's right," he declared noticing the worried look on Janice's face. "Don't worry. We've got the funds to buy this place."

"No, I'm not worried. I'm sure you have a letter of pre-qualification from your lender."

"Nope."

"No? I was under the impression that you were pre-qualified."

Maggie smiled. "Quit giving her a bad time, Jack."

"This is a cash deal, Janice. We're not financing," he told her.

"Oh," Janice exclaimed, surprised. "For some reason, I thought you were financing." She grinned. "Well, cash is even better."

"We won a lottery, Janice," Maggie said. "A few months ago, we bought a single lottery ticket and hit a big one. It was the first time we played in over a year and we had all the right numbers. I still can't believe it."

"Lucky you," Janice said. "It must be nice to not have to worry about money."

"It is. It really is," Maggie replied. "Jack and I have worked our butts off for years just to keep our heads above water. Then, just like that, everything changed. It's like a dream, isn't it, honey?"

"I'm still pinching myself to be sure I'm awake. But, it's true, all right. We're richer than shit."

Chapter Two

"What time is the delivery due?" Beth asked Dr. Angela Simmons.

"I expect them any minute now. The gate is locked, so they'll have to use the intercom to let us know they are here."

"Do you know the count?"

Angela shrugged. "I was told ten donations, but sometimes that number changes due to unforeseen circumstances. Whatever it is, I'll be glad for some new sites to work. This will be the first time we will have a mass grave to study. It should be extremely interesting to watch the degree of decomposition."

"Are you putting all of them in one grave?"

"No. Probably six. We also want to do a study of bodies encased in concrete, so we'll use a couple of cadavers for that," Angela told her.

"Will you bury the bodies you're putting in concrete at different depths?" Beth asked.

Angela smiled. "That's right. Good for you."

"I listen. How many years will you leave them buried before you dig them up?" Beth inquired

"It depends on a lot of factors, but I'm sure it will be three years or longer." Angela glanced out of the window. "There's a doe over there," she declared.

"Is there a fawn with her?" Beth asked. "I've seen a doe with her baby a few times this week."

"No, she's alone," Angela told her.

"What about the other two bodies?" Beth asked, as she walked over to the window and looked at the deer.

"They will be submerged in water."

"You're not talking about the lake, are you?" Beth inquired.

"Of course not. We'll put them in that pond on the west side of the property that Jason dug out a couple of weeks ago. It's full now, so we can use it."

"It took a long time to fill it," Beth stated.

"It's a big pond."

"How many cadavers will you have after today's delivery?"

"Forty-one or two, depending on what they bring us today."

"That seems a lot," Beth said.

"Not really. We're still new and growing. We'll be adding more over time. There's no end to the scenarios we can explore. I think we're now the second largest body farm in the country, size-wise. However, there are smaller farms that have more cadavers than us."

"Texas has the biggest body farm."

"It does, as far as acreage is concerned. I'm not sure if they have more cadavers in the field than some of the other farms though. And, remember, the cadavers are replaced with new ones after the students are done with them so the number is constantly changing."

"That's right. The cadaver I worked on had been buried for over two years. It was an older woman who had been beaten to death. Her body was reclaimed by the family after we were finished with her."

"That happens on occasion, but usually the bones stay with us. By the way, Beth, your internship will be over in a couple of weeks. Have you ever considered learning forensic facial reconstruction?"

"I've thought about it, but I'm not sure that's the route I want to take."

"You should consider it. I think you'd be very good at it."

"Thanks. I will consider it," Beth replied. "Did you hear that the property next to the farm has been sold?" she asked, changing the subject.

"That place south of us?" Angela replied.

"Yeah, that's the one."

"I thought that they were going to divide it and sell off parcels," Angela declared.

"I heard that, too. However, just one person bought it all. There's like ..." She thought for a moment. "I heard it's around forty-some acres."

"That sounds about right. It's about twice the size of our farm. Do you know who bought it? Not another nudist colony, I hope."

Beth grinned. "Nope. I heard it was just a regular family with a lot of money."

"That's a big house. How many kids?"

"A couple of teenage boys."

"I hope that doesn't become a problem," Angela said. "Teenagers can be curious animals."

"I doubt they'll try anything. There are enough warning signs to stay off the property, plus that razor fencing is certainly a deterrent."

"Unless they come by sea," Angela said, grinning.

"There's even more no trespassing signs along the lakeshore."

"I've got a couple of cadavers in that area, not too far from the lake. I certainly wouldn't want a couple of kids coming across them."

Beth grinned. "It would probably scare the pants off of them. If you want, I'll go over there tomorrow and make sure all the warning signs are visible."

"Thanks, Beth. That's a good idea."

"There's the intercom," Beth exclaimed. "It looks like our delivery is here."

Dr. Simmons made the sign of the cross, closed the refrigerator door, and sighed heavily. Although she appreciated the fact that the donor list was longer than the FBI may ever need, she still had a problem trying to understand how someone could donate their body to a body farm. They must know that their cadaver would be left to rot away over the years, and yet there were still hundreds of people who donated every year.

She could understand donating eyes or a heart or some organ that would sustain or better a person's life. However, to be buried, hung from a tree, placed in the trunk of a car, or just sprawled out in a shallow grave to have the insects, birds, and animals chew you up while you're decomposing was something else.

She pulled off her gloves and mask, took a deep breath, and walked outside. It was warm, but there was a comforting breeze blowing in from the north and Angela closed her eyes and let it sweep over her for a few moments. "I'd die for a cigarette," she mumbled. *Funny,* she thought, *how the desire has never gone away after all this time.* She turned when she saw Beth walking towards her.

"It's getting hot," Beth stated.

"It's that time of year," Angela replied. "A couple more days and we'll be hearing fireworks."

"I guess. Those bare-assed naturalists do like to celebrate."

Angela laughed. "They do, indeed."

"We have a group of students coming next week, don't we?"

"We do. Five young eager persons will be here, who have no idea that they will be gagging and retching while they locate and inspect the remains of these poor dead people."

"I remember the first cadaver that I found when I was a student. It was on the body farm down in Texas," Beth said softly.

"Did it get to you?"

Beth grinned. "That's putting it mildly. I tossed my cookies more than once. I'll never forget the smell. It was horrible. Now I barely notice it."

"Well," Angela said, "it's supposed to be hotter than blazes next week. The smell will be overpowering, to say the least."

"I'll make sure that the students have some barf bags with them. We sure don't want them throwing up on the cadavers and spoiling the site."

Chapter Three

"That's it. Give me your phones," Maggie Keegan said, as she reached towards the back seat of the SUV.

"Ahh, Mom. I didn't do anything," Alex, her twelve-year-old son, whined.

"Phone. Now. You, too, Michael."

"What the hell did I do," Michael shouted. "I'm not giving you my phone."

Jack Keegan pulled the SUV over to the side of the road and threw it into park. "I've had it with you two," he yelled as he turned and looked at his two sons. "You've had your noses stuck in those phones since we left. It's enough. Now, give your mother your phones." He stared at Michael. "As for you, young man, if I ever hear you swear at your mother again, there'll be big trouble. Understand?"

"I didn't," Michael yelled.

"Michael, don't argue with me. You did and I don't want it to happen again."

"Why can't we just go back home? I don't want to move. I want to stay with my friends."

"Yeah, me, too," Alex moaned. "This is bull."

"Phones," Maggie said. She waited for a moment. "Don't make me tell you again," she threatened.

Michael threw his phone into the front seat, barely missing his mother's head. "Happy now?" he asked sarcastically.

"That's two weeks without your phone, Michael," Jack told him. "How about you, Alex? Do you want to throw your phone at your mother, too?"

"This is so bogus," Michael muttered, slouching down in the seat.

"Here," Alex said, handing his mother his phone.

"Thank you," Maggie said.

"Okay, everyone out," Jack yelled.

"What?" Alex asked, perplexed at the order to get out of the SUV.

"You heard me. Out!" Jack opened his door and stepped onto the pavement. He walked around the vehicle and opened his wife's door. "Maggie," he said, taking her hand and helping her out. "Now, you two," he ordered, opening the door.

The two boys slowly vacated the back seat, looking worried. "Now you've done it," Alex whispered to Michael.

"Everybody breathe," Jack said. "I want all of you to take a few deep breaths and relax. You two are acting as though moving to a new home is a death sentence. You need to open up your minds and allow the experience of new things to come in. This is a good thing we're doing. I know you are upset because you had to leave your friends behind, but you can stay in touch with them. Next summer, if you want, you can invite some of them to come and stay with you for a week or two. I just want you to give it a chance. If you hate your new school and living in your new home – well, after a few months, we'll make other arrangements for you. I just want you to keep an open mind. This is something your mother and I want for you boys and we hope you can appreciate it."

"What other arrangements?" Michael asked.

"What?"

"You said you'd make other arrangements. What are they? Will we move back to Chicago?"

"Oh, no. That's not an option. However, your mother and I talked it over and decided that if you don't want to live in your new home – if you really, really hate it - we'll send you to military school. That way, you'll only have to put up living with us three months out of the year instead of twelve. Although ..." He hesitated.

"What?" Michael asked.

"Well, I understand that in certain circumstances, boys can live there year-round and only go home for the holidays. But you don't have to visit, of course. I mean, I would understand if you don't. After all, who would want to visit such a horrible place like your new home?"

"Mom?" Alex cried out. "I don't want to go to military school. Please don't make me."

"Well, we'll just have to wait and see how it goes, won't we?" she told him.

"Now, should we all get back in the car and enjoy the rest of the trip to our new home?" Jack asked. "I want you boys to look at the scenery. It's a beautiful world we live in and I don't want you to miss it."

"Can I have my phone back?" Alex asked.

"After we get to our new house," Maggie told him.

"What about me?" Michael asked.

"Two weeks, Mikey. And, you can't borrow Alex's phone to call your friends. Understand?" Jack told him.

"Besides, you'll be so busy enjoying your new surroundings, you'll probably forget all about that phone," Maggie added.

"I doubt it," Michael muttered.

"Now that I think about it, I'm not even sure there is cell phone reception out by the new house. We may have to get a landline," Jack said, grinning. "Wouldn't that be a kick in the pants?"

"What?" Michael yelled. "Mom? Is he joking?"

Maggie shrugged. "I guess we'll find out, won't we?"

"Okay," Jack said, grinning. "Everyone, back in and buckle up. We still have a couple of hours before we get there."

Maggie waited a moment "All right, boys," she said quietly. "What happens from this point on is up to you. I suggest you spend the next couple of hours thinking about it."

"We made good time," Jack said as he turned onto Twisted Tree Road.

"Are we there?" Alex asked, looking out the window.

"Just about. Our house is just up the road." Jack slowed down and glanced over the area, watching for the drive to the house.

"Is that it?" Michael asked pointing to a house on the left side of the road. "It's not that big."

"No, Mike, that's the Sullivan house. Ours is just a little farther."

"Where is it?" Michael inquired. "I don't see..."

"Here," Jack said, stopping in the middle of the road. He turned and looked at the two boys in the back seat. "Are you ready to see your new home? Alex?"

"Go already," Alex replied.

"Mike. How about you?"

"Yeah, I guess."

"Okay, boys, here we go." He drove a few more feet, turned left into the driveway, and pulled up in front of the house.

"Wow!" Alex exclaimed, his mouth dropping open in surprise. "It's big." He glanced over at his mother. "Is this really our house?"

Maggie grinned. "It certainly is." She looked back at Michael. "Well, Mike, what do you think?"

Michael glanced toward her and then looked back at the house. "It's a mansion," he uttered softly. "It's a fucking mansion." He looked at his dad, fear written all over his face. "I'm sorry," he cried out. "I'm really sorry. Please, Dad, don't - Seriously, I'm sorry. I didn't mean to say that in front of mom. It just slipped out," he said, looking like he was about to cry.

"Forget it. I said the same thing when I saw it for the first time," Jack told him.

"Can we go in?" Alex asked softly.

"Absolutely. Come on, boys. It's time to introduce you to your new home."

"I can't believe how big it is," Alex commented as he got out of the SUV. "What are all those other buildings for?" he asked.

"Mostly storage. The pool equipment is in the smaller building. The lawn maintenance stuff is in one of the other ones. I forget which."

Michael punched Alex on the arm. "Did you hear that? There's a pool."

"I heard," he said grinning. "This is great, Mike."

Jack looked at Maggie. "Do you remember which building has the dirt bikes?"

Michael stared at him. "Dirt bikes? We have dirt bikes?"

"No way!" Alex shouted, falling to the ground laughing.

"Your mom and I thought it would be a good way for you to get around on the property. It's a long hike to the lake if you want to go fishing or boating, so we bought you each a bike. Tomorrow we'll go over the dos and don'ts and you can learn how to drive them," Jack told them.

"We have our own lake?" Michael asked, looking surprised.

"Well, I'm sure we share it, but we certainly have some of it on our land."

"I don't know how to fish," Alex said.

"You'll learn," Maggie said. "We'll teach you."

"We had a bunch of trees cleared out to make it easier to get to the lake, but it's still a pretty rough terrain. You're going to have to take it slow," Jack informed them. "We will also go over the rules about using the pool. But all that can wait. Let's go in so you can see your rooms."

Michael didn't move. He stared up at the huge house, looking confused.

"What's the problem, Mikey?" Maggie asked him.

"Why didn't you tell us?"

"Tell you what?" Maggie inquired.

"About all this. You made it sound like we were moving to a shack in the woods. Why didn't you tell us about all this?

"And, miss the looks on your faces?" Maggie replied, laughing. "Besides, Mike, it shouldn't have made a difference what size the house is. Our being together is the important thing."

"Just how big is it?"

"The house? It's pretty darn big," she told him.

"No, everything."

"Let's just say that you could get lost real easy without ever leaving our property. We're sitting on around forty acres of land, most of which have never been walked on," Jack told him.

"Not even by the Indians?" Alex asked.

"Well, maybe years ago the Indians were here," Jack said smiling. "As I said, there are going to be rules about all this. But that can wait. Come on. Let's get inside and get settled."

"What color are the bikes?" Alex asked.

Maggie grinned. "I believe there's a blue one and a green one. Right, Jack?"

"I call dibs on the blue one," Alex cried out.

"I want the green one," Michael yelled at the same time.

"Well, how about that, Jack? No argument. I wish everything was so simple."

Chapter Four

"So, where are you boys off to today?" Maggie asked as she cleared away the breakfast dishes. "Fishing, again?"

"We're tired of fishing from the shore. We never catch any fish. We want to take the boat out. Do you think dad would mind?" Michael told her.

"Would I mind what?" Jack asked as he walked into the kitchen.

"Can we take the boat out?" Michael asked.

"I don't think so, Mike. We talked about this and I don't want you and Alex going out by yourselves yet. I want to go out with you a few times and make sure you guys know what you're doing before you go off on your own."

"I know. But you've said that every day for the past two weeks. When are you gonna show us?"

"How about we plan on Saturday? I'll save the whole day to spend with you guys. We can go fishing and I'll let you guys drive the boat and see how you do. Fair enough?"

"I guess," Michael replied. He glanced over at his mother. "Can I make some sandwiches to take with us? Alex and I are going to see if we can explore the whole shoreline."

"That's a lot of land to cover," Jack said. "Just be sure you stay on our property and don't wander off and get lost."

"And, you boys make sure you have your walkie-talkies with you," Maggie told them.

"Yes, mom," Michael and Alex said in unison.

"And, look out for bears," Jack told them, grinning.

"Which way do you want to go?" Alex asked Michael.

Michael looked at the water and shrugged. "You choose. I gotta pee." He got off his bike, walked a few feet away from the shore, and stood behind a tree.

"Hurry up," Alex yelled after a few minutes.

"I'm coming," Michael yelled back.

"We're going to go right," Alex told Michael as he got back on his bike.

"The brush is too thick," Alex said thirty minutes later. "We're never going to get through it on these bikes. We better turn back."

"No way. I want to see what's over there. I think I hear something."

"We can't get through on the bikes, Mike. Anyway, that noise could be a long way from us. Sounds travel a lot farther across water."

"Where did you hear that?"

"I read it somewhere. If you're out in the middle of a lake in a boat talking, people on the shore can hear you," Alex replied.

"That's crazy. I never heard that." He looked around the area, considering their options. "How about we leave the bikes here and walk it? As long as we follow the shoreline, we won't get lost."

"I don't know," Alex said, wavering between going back towards their home or seeing where the noise was coming from.

"Come on, Alex."

"If anything happens, Dad will kill us."

"What can go wrong? We'll walk on the edge of the lake until we get there," Michael said.

"All right. But, if it gets bad, we go back. Okay?"

"Okay," Michael replied.

"Promise," Alex asked.

"I promise. Come on, let's go see where the noise is coming from." Michael took a few steps and stopped.

"What's the matter?" Alex asked him.

"I almost forgot our sandwiches and water."

"Look," Michael whispered. "Over there."

"What?"

"There's a fence over there with a sign on it. This must be the end of our property."

"What does the sign say? Can you read it?" Alex asked.

"I think it says no trespassing, but I can't see it that good."

"Do you hear something?"

"Shh." Michael listened for a minute. "I can hear people talking."

"Get down," Alex told him, pulling on Michael's shirt as he bent down trying to hide. "Look. There are people over there in the water."

Michael dropped down alongside his brother and stared at where Alex was pointing. Suddenly, he laughed.

"What?" Alex asked.

"I think they are all naked."

"What?" Alex asked, looking stumped. "Why would they be naked?"

"They are," Michael said excitedly. He punched Alex on the arm.

"Ouch, that hurt. Stop punching me already." Alex said, rubbing his arm.

"Look. Look, Alex. No one has any clothes on."

"I think we better get out of here," Alex said nervously. "What if they see us?"

"So what? We're not doing anything wrong. We're on our property."

"I think we should go, Mike."

"Let's get closer."

"No way. I'm not getting closer," Alex told him.

"If we were in our boat, we could see them better."

"Well, we're not, so let's go."

"I want to get a better look," Michael said. "You stay here if you want."

"No, wait," Alex cried out, as Michael walked away.

"Shh!" Michael said, turning and looking at Alex. "Be quiet. I'll be right back."

"Shit," Alex muttered, as he watched his brother walk away from him.

Alex jumped as Michael came up from behind him and touched his shoulder. "Shit, Mike, you scared the hell out of me."

"Don't be such a baby."

"I didn't even hear you coming."

"You should have come with me, Alex. I found a great hiding spot real close. I could see really good."

"We better head home. Mom's gonna be worried. We were supposed to check in with her."

"I could see everything. Some of the people were kinda fat but most of the women looked pretty good. I saw some great boobs, Alex, and almost everyone didn't have hair down there. I could see their pussies."

"You perv," Alex told him. "Who cares about that shit?"

Michael stared at him for a moment. "Yeah, sorry I forgot you're still a kid. One of these days, Alex, you'll be right there with me staring at those pussies."

"You're gross. Let's get out of here."

"I'm pretty sure it's a nudist camp," Michael told his brother.

"I never heard of that before. Is it like boy scout camp?"

Michael grinned. "I guess. Kinda, except it's for adults and they don't wear clothes."

"That's dumb," Alex said.

"Promise me you won't tell mom and dad about finding it."

"Don't you think that they should know naked people are living there?"

"They don't live there, Alex. It's like a place to come and vacation."

"Why would anyone want to vacation naked? I don't get it?"

"You will someday. Just promise me you won't tell. Okay?"

Alex shrugged. "I guess. I still don't get it, though."

"You boys had us worried. We were about ready to come and look for you."

"I'm sorry, Mom. We left the bikes to walk around by the lake and we forgot to take the walkie-talkies with us. It won't happen again."

"I certainly hope not. You're going to have to make sure you have them with you all the time, Michael."

"I will. I promise."

"Alex, you, too. Promise me you'll always have them with you so I can reach you."

"I promise, Mom."

"Good. Are you boys hungry?"

"I'm starving," Alex replied.

"How about you, Mike?" Maggie asked. "Do you want a snack?"

"No. I'm good. I'm gonna go take a shower," Michael told her, rushing out of the kitchen.

"He was sure in a hurry," Maggie said.

"We saw naked people," Alex stated.

"You saw what?" Maggie exclaimed. "Where in the world were you?"

"By the lake. Mike says it's a nudist camp. There were all kinds of naked people by the lake swimming and stuff."

Maggie stared at him, shocked at what she had heard. "Jack," she yelled. "Get in here!"

Jack hung up the phone and shook his head.

"What? Didn't you talk to her?" Maggie asked.

"It seems our realtor is still on vacation. However, her manager was very apologetic," he said. "A whole lot of good that does us now. Damn. This really pisses me off."

"Well, maybe it's not that bad, Jack. We just have to be sure that the boys don't go back there again."

"I don't like it, Maggie. Janice should have told us about that place before we bought this house."

Maggie grinned.

"What's so funny?" Jack asked.

"Now I get why Mike was in such a hurry to take a shower."

"Really? You think that's funny?" he asked, trying to hold back a smile.

"He's been in there so long the water must be cold by now. It's gotta be all shriveled up," Maggie said laughing"

"Our water bill is going to be huge," Jack stated, grinning.

"We live in the country, remember. We don't get a water bill," Maggie reminded him. She smiled. "Our boys are growing up, Jack. It's all part of the process."

"You're right. And, if you've noticed, Alex's voice is starting to change."

"I hope that well has a lot of water in it," Maggie said grinning.

"Okay. So, we agree this is no big deal. I'll talk to the boys about staying away from that area."

"Good," Maggie said.

"I just hope there isn't anything else that Janice forgot to mention."

Chapter Five

"I'm sorry, boys, but I don't have any control over the weather," Jack said. "We'll go out tomorrow if it clears up." He looked at the disappointment showing on his sons' faces and glanced over at Maggie. "How about we go for a ride into town? We'll make a day of it. Boys, do you want to do some shopping?"

"For what?" Alex asked, still pouting over the fact that they couldn't go boating.

"School is starting in a few weeks. You need some new school clothes. We can check out the stores and see what they've got." He glanced over at Maggie. "I want to order a couple more dirt bikes for you and me."

"Oh, Jack, I'm not sure I want a bike," Maggie declared.

"Of course, you do. We'll get a black one and a white one. That way we can all ride together. Besides, we should have a few more bikes for when the boys' friends come over. I need some chemicals for the pool, too. Maybe, I should make a list."

"No need. I'll remember," Maggie told him.

He looked at Michael. "How about we have lunch at that restaurant you're always talking about?"

"The Meat and Eat Diner?" Michael said. "Yeah, let's eat there. I heard it's great."

"Where'd you hear that from?" Alex asked. "You don't know nobody from around here."

"I looked it up on the internet. It has great reviews."

"Okay, then. Lunch at The Meat and Eat Diner it is," Jack said.

"Sounds good," Maggie said. "Boys, you need to change before we leave."

"Why? What's wrong with what I'm wearing?" Alex whined.

"Your pants are filthy. Now, go change and throw those in the wash." She glanced at Michael. "You, too."

"Ah, Mom, my pants are clean," Michael told her.

"You heard your mother," Jack said. "Go change your clothes."

"How come you always take mom's side?" Alex asked.

"Because she's the one who cooks my meals, that's why."

Alex glanced over at Michael. "What's that got to do with anything?"

Michael looked at his father. "Should I tell him?"

"Go ahead."

"Because he's afraid she'll poison his food if he doesn't agree with her," Michael told Alex.

"She wouldn't do that!" Alex exclaimed. "Would you, Mom?"

"He's joking, you idiot," Michael told Alex. "It's a joke."

"Well, I don't see what's funny about that," Alex declared.

"Forget it," Michael said. "Let's go change."

Jack pulled out of the driveway and turned left.

"You're going the wrong way," Maggie told him.

"I want to take a look at something," Jack said. "It's not far." He was quiet as he drove down Twisted Tree

Road watching for a turn. He slowed down and made a left onto Yellow Snake Road.

"Where are you going?" Maggie asked.

"Just looking around," Jack said. He drove a little further and pulled the car over to the side of the road. "Well, I guess Mike was right," he declared as he looked at a sign on the other side of the road.

"I can't read that sign. What does it say?" Maggie asked.

"It says that this is an entrance to The Twisted Tree Nature Club. Should we drive in and take a look around?" he asked, grinning. "Maybe you should put your glasses on so you can see."

"Jack Keegan, you turn this car around. We are not going to take a look," Maggie said, holding back a smile. "And, I can see just fine."

"Yeah, Dad, let's go in and take a look," Michael exclaimed.

"That's enough, Mike." Maggie stared at Jack. "Well, do you plan on sitting here all day?"

"I thought we were going to town," Alex said. "Why are you being such a perv, Dad? I thought Mike was the only perv in this family."

Jack did a uey and drove back towards Twisted Tree Road. "I just wanted to see for myself what was there, Alex. You don't have to worry about me being a perv. Mike is the only perv in this family. Right, Mikey?"

"Real funny, Dad."

"You boys just make sure you stay away from that place," Maggie said. "Do you hear?"

"You told us already," Michael replied.

"Well, I'm telling you again." She glanced over at Jack. "That goes for you, too."

26

Jack grinned. "Yes, ma'am. I hear you. Oh, I almost forgot. You boys will have to stay close to the house for the next few days. I'm having some of the trees cleared out and I don't want to be worrying about you being in the woods while it's going on," Jack said."

"Where at?" Michael asked.

Jack stopped, checked for traffic, and turned onto Twisted Tree Road. "Actually, they are going to be clearing on the northwest side of the property. It's too overgrown for you boys to be able to ride around over there. After we get some of those dead trees and brush cleared away, you'll have a whole new area to explore."

"Good, keep them on that side," Maggie mumbled.

"What was that?" Jack asked her.

"Nothing, dear," she said smiling. "What about the other thing? Are you going to tell them?"

"Well, that's more for us than the boys," Jack replied.

"I'm sure they'll use it, too," Maggie told him.

"What's that, Dad?" Alex asked.

"I'm putting in a tennis court."

"Wow! That's great, Dad," Alex said excitedly. "I always wanted to learn how to play. Will you teach me?"

"Of course."

"You know what I think is a good idea, Dad?" Michael asked.

"What's that?"

"As long as those guys are going to be putting down a bunch of concrete, why don't we put in a basketball court, too?"

"Let's not get carried away, Mike. I think the basketball hoop next to the driveway is sufficient."

"I guess. It was just an idea."

"So, are you boys excited about school starting in a few weeks?" Maggie asked, trying to nudge the subject away from the basketball court.

"Kinda," Michael said. "I'm kinda nervous, too."

"I can't wait," Alex said.

"Well, I'm sure you'll both make lots of new friends." Maggie looked over at Jack. "Can you believe Mike is starting high school? Where has the time gone, Jack?"

"I know. Before we know it, the boys will be married with a bunch of kids and we'll be a couple of old white hairs."

Maggie smiled. "Let's not rush it, Jack. And, in case you haven't noticed, you've already sprouted a few white hairs."

"I ain't getting married," Alex muttered. "No way."

"We'll see," Maggie said, laughing.

"What about fishing, Dad?" Michael asked.

"What about it?"

"Can we still go fishing while the woods are being cleared out?"

"I don't think that's a good idea. It won't hurt you to stay around the house for a few days."

"I guess," Michael said and looked at his phone. "Hey, I got a text from Bud."

"What did he say?" Alex asked.

"What do you care?"

"I don't. He's dumb, anyway," Alex said, turning away and looking out the window.

"Did the tree guys say how long they would be here?" Maggie asked Jack.

"It's a big job. I figure it will take ..." He glanced over at the front door. "Somebody's here," he said.

"I'll get it." Maggie walked over to the door and opened it.

"Are you the one having those trees cut down?" a man yelled.

Maggie stared at him. "Jack," she exclaimed, "would you come over here?"

Jack walked over to the door and smiled at an elderly man standing on the front porch. "Is there something I can help you with?" he asked.

"You can stop cutting down those trees."

"And, you are?"

"I'm Sullivan. Fred Sullivan. I live down the road."

"I'm glad to meet you. I'm Jack and this is my wife, Maggie. Would you like to come in?"

"What I'd like is for those men to quit cutting down those trees," he shouted. "What the hell is wrong with you? Some of those trees have been here over a hundred years and you think you can just come in here and cut them down? They're landmarks, for God's sake."

"Mr. Sullivan, would you like to begin again? I have no idea what you are talking about."

"The trees. The twisted trees. They've been like that since a tornado went through here over a century ago." He looked at Jack and frowned. "You really don't know what I'm talking about, do you?"

"I don't," Jack said, shaking his head. "Why don't you tell me?"

"Please, Mr. Sullivan," Maggie said. "Come in and have a cup of coffee with us. Perhaps, you can explain to us what you're talking about."

Fred Sullivan looked at her, trying to decide what to do. "I could go for a cup of coffee," he told her and walked in. "Where's the kitchen?"

Jack sat back in his chair. "I had no idea," he told Fred. Our realtor conveniently forgot to discuss some things with us."

Fred grinned. "You shoulda asked."

"Right," Jack agreed. "And, how often do you ask your realtor if there are twisted trees on the property?"

"Or, if you have nudists vacationing on the property next to you," Maggie added, smiling.

"How long have you lived here, Fred?" Jack asked.

"Oh, a long time now. Lucy and I raised our two boys here. They've moved now, of course." He thought for a moment. "My God, it's been fifty years already. This was our first house and it will be our last, I guess." He sighed. "It's been a good house."

"More coffee?" Maggie asked him.

"Just a shot and then I've got to get going. Lucy will be wondering what happened to me."

"We'd love to meet her. Do you think you'd like to come for dinner sometime?"

"Oh, I don't know," Fred said. "We're kinda simple folks. I don't know if our stomachs could handle your fancy cooking."

Jack grinned. "There's no fancy food cooked here; I can assure you. We grill out a lot. Do you think you and Lucy could handle a burger or a brat?"

"Now you're talking. Just let us know when."

"Next Wednesday," Maggie told him. "How about six o'clock?"

Fred grinned. "That sounds great. We'll be here." He stood up and walked towards the door. "I'm sorry I yelled at you," he said. "It's just those trees mean a lot to the people around here."

"No worries. As I said, we didn't plan on felling any living trees. We just want to clear out the dead stuff. Now that we know about those twisted trees, we'll take a hike through the woods and check them out. You said there are about a dozen of them. Right?"

"Fourteen," Fred replied. "Well, maybe less than that, but at least eleven. I don't know if any are left on the FBI's property. There were a couple of trees there at one time but I can't get over there to check it out. I do know that vacant lot next to you had three of them last time I checked."

"Excuse me, did you say the FBI has property here?" Maggie asked.

"Yeah, they own a piece of land just north of me. Anyway, as I said, I'm not sure how many of the trees are left. Maybe we can go out and do a count someday," Fred continued.

"The boys will be interested in them. They enjoy discovering new things," Maggie declared.

"If you get out on the lake, check the shoreline. There are a few of those trees by the water," Fred said.

"Thanks, I'll do that. Are there any on your property?" Jack asked him.

"Not anymore. I had a few but they died off a few years ago. I doubt the ones still standing will last much longer but we need to take good care of them."

"Indeed, we do. It was good meeting you, Fred. We'll see you on Wednesday."

"Nice old guy," Jack said, as he closed the door and walked back into the kitchen.

"He was, once he stopped yelling at us." Maggie picked up the dirty cups and put them in the dishwasher. "Well, that was interesting," she stated. "We have the FBI living near us. I wonder if there are any more surprises."

"So, the FBI owns some land here. Big deal. You know, Mags, I've seen some of those trees. They are weird-looking. I never even gave it a second thought or wondered why they looked like that," Jack said. "He's right. They are scattered all over the place."

"I've got to look this up on the internet," Maggie told him. "Who would imagine that a tornado could twist trees like that? You'd think they would have been pulled right out of the ground and blown away, not twisted. There has to be a different explanation, don't you think?" She glanced over at Jack. "Are you listening to me?"

"Of course."

Maggie shook her head. "No, you're not."

"I was. I have a great idea, Mags."

Maggie rolled her eyes and sighed. "God, help me. Now what?"

"Let's see if the property east of us is for sale."

"You mean that wooded lot? What would we want that for?"

"We could make it into a nature walk and open it up to the public."

Maggie laughed. "Maybe we can get the FBI to sell their land to us, too. And, the Sullivan family may want to part with their property. However..." She thought for a moment.

"What?"

"I wouldn't mind buying that nudist camp and tearing it down. Just, think, Jack. We could own it all."

"You don't have to get cute. It was just an idea."

"I'll be in the den," Maggie replied. "I want to check out Fred's story."

Chapter Six

"What do you think is back there?" Alex asked his brother.

"How should I know?" Michel got off his dirt bike and walked over to the fence.

"Don't touch it!" Alex yelled. "It might be electrified."

Michael hesitated and pulled his arm back. "I doubt it, but somebody sure doesn't want us going there. Let's see where it goes. Maybe, there's a house back there."

"Let's go back, Mike," Alex said. "I don't like it here."

"Come on. We'll only walk a little way. There's nothing to be afraid of."

Alex stayed on his bike. "I'm going fishing."

"I think it's gonna rain."

"Let's just go back home."

"I wanna see what's back there, Michael repeated."

"I don't feel like it. I'll wait for you here," Alex said, not moving. "The lake is right over there. Maybe, I'll throw my line in and see if I can catch anything."

"Have you got that pocket pole with you?"

"So, what if I do?" Alex replied.

"Nothing." Michael started walking away. "You sure you don't want to come?" he asked.

"It's getting pretty windy, Mike. I think it's gonna rain. We should go back."

"I won't go far. You stay right around here, okay?"

34

"Don't worry. I'm not gonna get lost." Alex said.

"You better not. Mom would kill me if anything happened to her baby."

"Shut up, you freak," Alex yelled.

"See ya," Michael said, as he started walking west following the fence line.

"Michael, calm down. You're not making any sense," Jack said.

"A body. I saw a dead body. You need to call the cops," Michael told him, his body shaking. "It was ..."

"You found a body?" Maggie interrupted. "Are you sure? Where?"

"Here. Take a drink of water," Jack told him. He handed the glass to Michael and watched as he took a long drink of water. "Now, very slowly, tell us again what you think you saw."

"I smelled it before I saw it," Michael said. "I thought it was some animal that had died. I was by the fence and I looked towards the smell and I saw a body lying on the ground." He took a deep breath and let it out. "It was about twenty or thirty feet away from the fence. It was kinda buried, but I could see part of it sticking out of the dirt."

"It was on the other side of the fence? Right?" Jack asked.

"Right. I was just walking along trying to see if there was a house or something over there when I saw it."

"Jack, what do you think? That area belongs to the FBI, doesn't it?" Maggie asked her husband.

"I think we should call the police. If Michael says he saw a body, I believe him."

"Where's Alex?" Maggie asked Michael. "Didn't he come back with you?"

"Oh, crap," Michael exclaimed. "I forgot about him. He wasn't with me when I found the body. He was fishing."

"You left him out there all alone?" Maggie exclaimed. "How could you do that, Michael?"

"I'm sure he's fine, Maggie. Just call him on the walkie-talkies and tell him to come home."

"He doesn't have them. I had them with me," Michael told her.

Maggie stared at Jack. "What should we do?"

"First of all, Maggie, don't panic." He glanced over at Michael, "You come with me. We're gonna go get Alex. Do you know where he is?"

"Yeah, but you don't need to come, Dad. I'll go get him."

"No, I'm coming with you. Maggie, you call the police and ask them to drive out here. We should be back in a few minutes."

"What should I tell them?" Maggie asked.

Jack looked at her and shrugged. "I don't know. Just tell them to keep the sirens off. There's no need to scare anyone."

"You'll come right back, won't you? I'm worried about Alex."

Jack smile. "Of course, and there's nothing to be worried about. Alex is fine."

"Are you friggin' kidding me," Jack yelled.

"Jack, your language," Maggie exclaimed.

"Screw my language," Jacked shouted. "First a nudist camp and now this! I'm suing that damn real

36

estate agent. Isn't there such a thing as disclosure when you buy property?" He stared at the cop. "Well? Isn't there?"

"I'm sorry, sir," Deputy Downing told him, "but you'll have to ask your attorney about that."

"Excuse me," Maggie interrupted, "but what is a body farm?"

"Really, Maggie?"

"I want to know," she told him.

"It is land owned by the FBI where bodies are disposed of using different scenarios and are studied over a period of time. Students training to be FBI agents come to the farm to learn how insect infestation, the weather, animal, and bird scavenging, and ..."

"That's enough, Deputy," Maggie exclaimed. "I get the picture."

"That's cool," Michael mumbled.

"It's gross," Alex said.

"All right, boys, you can go to your rooms," Maggie said.

"Ah, Mom," Michael whined.

"I said you're both excused. Out." She waited a moment while the boys left the room. "Deputy Downing, would you care for something to drink?" Maggie asked.

"No, thanks, ma'am. I'm good." He looked around the room and smiled. "This sure is a beautiful home you have here."

"Thank you."

"So, if there's nothing else, I'll be leaving now. I'm sorry I had to be the one to give you the bad news."

"It's not your fault, Deputy Downing," Jack said. "I appreciate you coming out."

"I see you put in a tennis court. And, please call me Dan. We're pretty informal around here."

"Dan, it is. Do you play tennis?" Jack asked him.

"A little. I used to be pretty good, but it's been a while."

"Well, come on out anytime and we'll play a few sets."

Dan grinned. "You serious? I'd love to."

"Like I said, anytime. Just give me a call."

"Please do," Maggie said, smiling at the Deputy. "He's constantly after me to play with him and I stink at it. The boys have just learned how to play and I can't even beat them. Please, come play with him."

"I'd love to. I've got a couple of days off next week. Would that work for you?" he asked Jack.

"Just tell me when and I'll be waiting and ready," Jack replied.

"I should warn you, Dan, he's very competitive and he hates to lose," Maggie said.

Jack hung up the phone and shook his head. "Well, Nelson says there is nothing we can do about it."

"You're kidding. Maybe we should talk to a different attorney. There must be something we can do about it."

"Nope. Janice was not required to inform us about the farm or the nudist camp. It was our responsibility to check this shit out ourselves before we bought the house."

"I wonder why Fred Sullivan didn't mention it when we were talking," Maggie mumbled.

"He's old. He probably didn't even think about it."

"You know, Jack, the body farm doesn't bother me that much."

Jack stared at her. "You're kidding," he exclaimed. "I don't get you at all."

"But, that nudist camp ticks me off big time. I don't like the boys being subjected to that type of lifestyle. I just don't think it's right."

"So, dead bodies scattered all over one place is okay but a few live ones running around naked somewhere else, where no one can see them, is what bothers you."

"It does when they're visible to the boys. They grow up fast enough as it is. I don't like them being this close to that filth."

"It's not really filth, Mags. It's a lifestyle for some people. It isn't against the law."

"It should be."

"Well, I guess we can always sell this place and live somewhere else. Maybe we should move further south, where it's warm all year round."

"No way. I love it here and so do the boys. No, I've got a better idea."

"Really?" he asked, wondering what was going through her mind.

She grinned. "Yes, really. How about we buy them out and shut it down?"

Jack laughed. "Yeah, right. I didn't know it was for sale," he said.

"It isn't, as far as I know. But we could make them an offer they couldn't refuse," Maggie said, smiling.

Jack stared at her. "You're serious," he declared.

"Dead serious. One way or the other, those people have got to go."

He thought for a few seconds. "Well, I guess if you don't ask, you don't know. How much do you think it will take?"

"Let's crunch some numbers. First, I'd like to see if I can get a look at the camp's financials. That might be available on the internet," Maggie told him. "Also, we need to find out who the owners are and what kind of financial shape they're in." She stood up and grinned.

"What?"

"Let's take a ride. Maybe, it's time to see what that place looks like from the inside, Mr. Vader."

"Mr. Vader? That's my name now?"

"Well, we don't want to use our real names, do we?"

"You're crazier than a bedbug, you know that?"

"You can be Vance and I'll be Ella," she said, excitedly. "We're Vance and Ella Vader," she declared, laughing.

He looked toward the ceiling and closed his eyes. "Oh, dear God, help me," he mumbled. "How long have you been waiting to use that?" he asked her.

"Just you never mind. Come on, let's go, Vance."

"I'm right behind you, Ella" Jack told her, laughing.

Chapter Seven

Dr. Angela Simmons ended the phone call. "Damn!" she yelled. She raised her arm but managed to stop herself before she threw her phone across the room. Chad looked over at her, concerned about the phone call she'd just had with her boss.

"No go?" he asked her.

"Nope. We're on the list, but it's a long list. Because our farm is so new, we are at the bottom. All the farms want to train cadaver dogs on their property, but there seems to be a shortage of dogs. How the hell can there be a shortage of dogs? Dogs are put down every day because nobody wants them, yet I'm told there aren't enough dogs to train."

"Well, it does take a special type of a dog to do that type of work," he stated.

"No shit," Angela blurted out. She turned and stared at Chad. "Oh, I'm so sorry, Chad. I didn't mean to use that language I'm just upset."

Chad smiled. "I've heard worse," he told her. He looked over at the intercom and listened.

"Who did they say it was?" Angela asked him.

Chad held up his hand, indicating for her to wait a moment. "I'm sorry," he said into the mike, "would you repeat that?"

"This is Jack Keegan. I live just south of your property. I'd like to talk to you."

"What is this about, sir?"

41

"About your stinking dead bodies, that's what."

Chad looked over at Angela and shrugged. "It's another person complaining. What should I do?"

Angela walked over and took the mike from Chad. "This is Dr. Simmons. What can I help you with?"

"It's about a body my son found," Jack hollered into the intercom.

"I suggest you notify the police if your son found a body, sir. That isn't what we do here."

"I know what you do here and I want to talk to you. Now, will you please open the gate so I can talk to you in person?"

"I'm sorry, but we don't allow civilians on the property."

Jack sat back in his car and took a deep breath. He leaned forward and exclaimed, "Okay. I get it. Perhaps it would be better if I come back here with the police."

"I'm afraid we can't allow them on the property either," Angela told him.

"I see. How about you come out to the gate, then, so we can talk face to face?"

"I'm sorry, but I only see people by appointment."

"Well, then, I'd like to make an appointment," Jack said.

"Can I ask what this is regarding?" Angela asked, looking at Chad and grinning.

"I told you. My son found a body on your property."

"That's a very serious statement, sir. If your son was on our property, I'm afraid we're going to have to have him arrested for trespassing."

"He wasn't exactly on your property. Oh, for God's sake, is there anyone there that I can talk to that has a brain?"

Angela clicked off her mike and glanced at Chad. "Too far?" she asked.

"I think you might want to stop," Chad told her.

"I guess," Angela said. She held the mike up to her mouth. "May I ask who you are?"

"I already told you my name. Are you about done messing around with me, Miss?" Jack asked her.

"Mr. Keegan, wasn't it? Jack Keegan?"

"That's right."

"If I understand what you're saying, Mr. Keegan, is that you're upset because your son was looking through the fence and saw one of our cadavers partially buried in the ground. You certainly can't be surprised about that. After all, we are an FBI body farm."

"I just found out about this farm being here a few days ago when he saw the body. I just want to ask if you can move those bodies farther away from the fence so people don't have to see that stuff. It was very traumatic for my son to see something like that."

"I understand your concern, Mr. Keegan. The local police already called us regarding your concerns. I'll tell you what we told them. From now on, we will try to place our cadavers so they can't be seen from the fence."

"I appreciate that," Jack said. "So, you'll ..."

"However," Angela interrupted, "there is nothing we can do about the bodies that are already buried close to the fence. Those will remain there until – well, until they don't."

"So, you won't move it?" Jack asked.

"It's not a question of won't. We can't. Once a cadaver is placed for study, it must remain there undisturbed. I'm sorry."

Without another word, Jack put his car in reverse and backed out of the driveway. "What a bitch," he mumbled. He pulled out his phone and called Maggie.

"So, did they agree to move that body?" she asked, as she answered her phone.

"I'm telling you, Maggie, that woman doctor is a real bitch. It took some talking but she finally agreed. You don't have to worry about any more bodies being buried where they can be seen," Jack told her. "Now, what's for lunch? I'm starving."

"You know you're in trouble if he reports you. You were way out of line," Chad told Angela.

"I know. I'm just sick of the complaints we keep getting. And, his kids shouldn't be sticking their noses through our fences. I still think we should wire it up."

"So, now you want to electrocute people," Chad declared. "Man, you are in a bad mood."

"Not kill them. Just a little jolt so they keep the hell away."

"I'm gonna go check cadaver seven."

"What's there to check?" Angela asked.

"I think he's too close to the edge of the water."

"He's not going to float away, Chad. His feet are buried in cement which is buried in the ground. He's staying right where he is."

"I'm gonna drive over there anyway. I need to get some fresh air."

"We have a meeting at ten. Be sure you're back in time."

"No problem," Chad replied, as he walked toward the door. He turned and looked back at Angela. "You know, I may be way out of line, but I think you need a vacation."

Angela stared at him. "You're right. You are out of line, Chad. It seems you tend to forget that while you're interning here, I'm your boss."

"I would never forget that. It's just that I'm worried about you."

Angela looked away and sighed. "I appreciate that. I guess I have been here too long without a break. I'll apologize to Mr. Keegan. Now run along and check on number seven."

Angela looked at the FBI trainees sitting around the large conference table. "Have any of you seen Chad?"

"I saw him this morning," a young student told her.

"No, I mean in the last half hour or so. He's not answering his phone. He said he would be ... Hold on, that might be him calling." She reached over, picked up her phone, and checked the caller ID. "Chad, where are you?"

"Angela?"

"Chad, where the hell are you?"

"You need to get down here right away."

"No. You need to get your butt back here for the meeting. Did you forget that ..."

"Angela, I found a body in the water," Chad interrupted. "You need to get down here."

"Really? It's a good thing you checked it out."

"No, it's not cadaver seven. I don't know who this is, Angela, but it isn't one of ours."

"How long do you think it's been in the water?" Chad asked.

45

"Not very long. Maybe a day or so."

"Should I call the police?"

"Wait. I'll have to check with headquarters. I'm not sure what the procedure is."

"Well, it's not one of ours and I did find it floating out there in the lake. I would think the local police would be the ones to handle this," Chad declared.

"I said wait," Angela told him. She looked down at the body that Chad had pulled onto the shore. "We probably shouldn't touch it again, but I want to get it up on the shore." She glanced over at the group of students who were observing what was going on. "Pete, come over here and help Chad pull this body the rest of the way out of the water. Charlotte, go back to the dorms and find an old blanket or something that we can cover this poor woman with."

"I'm not comfortable with that," Pete told her. "Have somebody else do it."

Angela stared at him, not believing her ears. "Are you afraid to touch a dead body, Pete?"

"It's not that. It's just that this is different from working on cadavers. It's creepy, that's all."

"Gloves," Angela said, reaching out to Chad. He handed her a pair of vinyl gloves and watched as she gloved up. "Ready?" Angela asked him.

"Ready," Chad told her. They reached down, grabbed the woman's arms, and pulled her onto the shore.

Angela glanced over at Pete. "My office at three. We need to talk."

"What for?"

"Just be there," Angela said.

46

Chapter Eight

Chief Ralph Wickers stared at the body and shook his head. "She doesn't look familiar. I can't remember seeing her around here. What about you, Deputy?"

"I've never seen her, Chief. Do you think she might be a member of that nudist camp across the lake?" Deputy Downing replied.

"That's my guess. We'll check them out."

"I'd appreciate it if your men could hurry up," Dr. Simmons said.

Chief Wickers glanced over at her and smiled. "We'll do our best, ma'am. Until the coroner and the ambulance get here there isn't a lot we can do. But you already know that, don't you?"

"I'm not trying to be rude," Angela told him. "It's just that we aren't supposed to have outsiders here. You know, you could accidentally disturb a location where we have a cadaver."

"We'll be careful and we'll get out of your hair as soon as possible."

"Thank you," Angela said. "Do you need me for anything else? I'd like to get back to work."

"I'll need statements from everyone who was at this spot after the body was found."

Angela looked over at him. "Everyone?"

"Yep."

"Well, I guess that would be everyone who works here on the farm. Chad found the body and called me. I rushed down here and ..." She thought for a moment. "All

47

the trainees were here, but I don't remember seeing Jason. He wasn't here."

"Who is Jason?" Chief Wickers asked her.

"He's our maintenance man. He does yard work and helps out wherever he's needed."

"Deputy Downing, I'll need statements from everyone. Dr. Simmons, can we use your facilities for this? It would be easier than taking statements down at the police station."

"Of course. There's a small conference room in the main building. Please, feel free to use it."

"Great. Deputy, how about you get started on taking the statements? And, make sure you talk to that Jason guy. He may have seen something."

"On it," Deputy Downing said, as he headed for his squad car. "Coroner's here," he yelled to Chief Wickers, as he opened his car door.

Chief Wickers turned off Yellow Snake Road onto the nudist camp's property and stopped. He looked around, determined that the large building to his right housed the office, and parked in front. Deputy Downing pulled in alongside him and got out of his car.

"You ever been here?" Wickers asked.

"A couple of times. Nothing serious and no arrests were made."

"What for?" Wickers asked him.

Downing laughed. "Both times were for fights between the same two men. It seems they couldn't agree on whether the ball was in or out."

"Tennis?"

"Nope. Volleyball. If you ever want to have nightmares, just try to break up a fight between two naked guys who can't agree on where the line is."

Wickers grinned. "I'll pass, thank you. Let's go in, shall we?"

An attractive blond glanced up from her desk and smiled as the two cops walked into the office. "Good afternoon," she said. "I'm Mandy. Can I help you?" She stood and extended her hand to Chief Wickers.

"That's fine, ma'am," he said, "we don't need to shake hands." He glanced over at Deputy Downing, who was staring at the woman and tried not to grin. "I was wondering if any of your members are missing."

"Missing? Not that I'm aware of," Mandy told him, smiling sweetly. "Why do you think someone's missing?"

"Is there some way you could check for me?" Wickers asked her.

"Could you wait just a moment? I'll get the manager." She stood up, walked across the room, and knocked on a door.

"Close your mouth, Dan," Wickers whispered. "You're drooling."

"She's naked, Chief."

"What did you expect? It's a nudist camp. You've been here before."

"Well, yeah. But that was a bunch of naked guys. I mean, look at her. She's absolutely ..."

"Mr. Bean will see you now, Deputy," Mandy called out, smiling.

"Thank you," Downing uttered, turning red in the face.

Chief Wickers and Deputy Downing waited until Mandy had walked back to her desk before they headed to the manager's office. Wickers knocked once and opened the door.

"Chief Wickers, good to meet you." An overweight, short, bald, naked man held out his hand. "I'm Robert Bean. Call me Red. All my friends call me Red. Mandy says you think one of our members may be missing. How can I help you?"

Wickers hesitated and then shook the man's hand. "How do you do? This is Deputy Downing. I'm sorry to inform you that a body was found in the lake this morning. The coroner estimates she was in there about twenty-four hours before she was found. We're just checking to make sure that all your members are accounted for."

"That's horrible," Red said, as he stood up and started pacing the room. "Absolutely horrible. Right here in our backyard, you say. A woman? How old?"

"Can you tell me if everyone is accounted for?" Chief Wickers asked, trying to avert his eyes as he spoke.

Red walked over to a small credenza and took out a bottle of bourbon. He looked over at the cops as he poured a drink. "You want one?" he asked them.

"No, thank you. We're on duty," Wickers answered. "Mr. Bean ..."

"Red, please. Call me Red."

"Red, would it be possible for you to sit back down?"

"Of course. Of course," Red said, as he waddled back to his deck and sat down. He grinned. "I sometimes forget I'm unclothed," he said. "Sorry, if it makes you uncomfortable."

THE TWISTED TREE TRIANGLE

"No, it's fine. However, if we could get on with this, I'd appreciate it. Do you mind?"

Red picked up a mike, pushed a button, and yelled. "I need a headcount, people. Women only. Please come to the main office now! All women. Please assemble at the main office immediately. Thank you." He looked at Wickers. "Give 'em a minute." He glanced down at a ledger. "We don't have many members here during the week. According to this," he said, indicating his ledger, "there should be sixteen – no, seventeen women here on the premises at this time."

Mandy opened the door and smiled. "I think the women are all here," she told Red.

"That was fast," Downing commented.

Chief Wickers and Deputy Downing followed Red out of his office and into a large vestibule. "Well, here they are," he told Wickers. "Did you ever see a finer-looking bunch of ladies?"

Wickers counted the woman and turned to Downing. "I count sixteen. How about you?"

"Sixteen, Chief. One's missing."

"No. There's seventeen," Red said. "You forgot about Mandy."

"I didn't realize she was included in your numbers. Okay, then. It looks like everyone is present and accounted for. Thank you for your time, ladies. Red, thanks for your help."

"No problem. Let me know if you hear anything."

I don't think I've ever been so uncomfortable," Wickers told Downing, as they walked back to their cars.

"There were some good-looking ladies there, Chief."

"Oh, the ladies were fine. It was Red who got to me. He should never take his clothes off. Never, ever. He should shower in them, sleep in them, everything – he should do everything dressed."

Downing grinned. "Did you notice he had no hair on his body? Not, anywhere. He must be a redhead, though, don't you think? I mean, his nickname is Red. Where else would he get a nickname ..."

"Enough, Deputy. And, no I didn't notice. I was trying not to look. Let's get out of here."

"Dinky's?"

"Damn right. I need a big stiff drink."

"Dinky's it is," Downing said. He opened his car door and got in. "We still have no idea who the woman is," he called over to Wickers.

"I'll meet you at the bar in twenty," Wickers yelled back, slamming his car door shut.

Chapter Nine

"Hey, Dan. Good to see you," Jack said as he opened the front door. "You don't look like you're dressed for tennis. What's up?"

"I wish that was why I'm here. Have you got a few minutes? I'd like to ask you and Maggie a couple of questions."

"Sure. Come on in. What's it about?"

"A body was found yesterday in Twisted Tree Lake. Some people over at the body farm pulled her out. No one seems to know who she is."

"Hold up a minute, Dan," Jack said. He turned towards the kitchen and yelled, "Maggie, can you come in here."

"What's up?" she asked as she walked into the room. She glanced over at Deputy Downing and smiled. "Hi, Dan. I didn't know you were here. Can I get you a cup of coffee?"

"No thanks," Downing replied.

"Dan's here on business, Mags," Jack told her. "It seems a body was found yesterday in the lake."

"Really?" She looked at Dan. "That's terrible. Who is it?"

"That's why I'm here. We're still trying to identify her." He reached into his pocket and pulled out a picture and handed it to Jack. "Do you recognize this woman? She'd been in the water for a while before this picture was taken, so it might be hard to tell."

Jack looked at the picture for a few seconds and handed it to Maggie. "I don't know her. How about you, Maggie?"

Maggie looked surprised as she glanced at the picture.

"Do you know her?" Deputy Downing asked.

Maggie shook her head no. "I'm sorry, but I don't know who it is. Poor thing." She hesitated as she started to hand the picture back to the deputy.

"Something else, Maggie?"

Maggie looked at the picture again. She shook her head no. "Sorry."

"No problem," Downing said. "Did either of you see any strange vehicles in the area Sunday or Monday?"

"Not that I recall."

"Me either, Dan," Maggie told him. "Although, the boys are outside more than we are and they may have seen something. I'll ask them and let you know."

"Thanks. I'd appreciate it."

"Can I ask how old she was?" Maggie asked.

"The coroner is still trying to determine her age, but we think she's between thirty and forty."

"It looks like she was very pretty," Maggie declared. "I gather it was an accident."

"Perhaps. We're not sure yet. She wasn't from around here and, so far, we haven't figured out what she was doing in the lake or how she got there." Downing headed for the door. "Well, I better get going. I need to stop at the Sullivan's and see if they saw anything."

"Good luck. Give me a call when you're free for a little tennis," Jack said.

"I'll do that," Downing said. "Take care."

Jack shut the door and frowned. "Well, what next?"

"Just stop, will you? I think we should find out if the boys saw anything. Will you go get them?"

"I'd just as soon not mention this to them right now. They'll hear about it sooner or later."

"Of course, they will. And, it will be something else for them to worry about. It's not enough that we have a body farm and a nudist camp next door. Now we've got to let them know that dead bodies are floating around in the lake."

"It's only one, Maggie. Don't get yourself all worked up."

"It's only one?" she yelled. "I think one is enough, don't you?"

"She definitely did not drown," Dr. Donna Dempsey told Chief Wickers.

"No water in her lungs?"

"Not enough to do any damage. No, she was dead when she was thrown in the lake."

"Do you know what killed her?" Wickers asked the coroner.

"She was strangled." She glanced up at Wickers. "Have you identified her yet?"

"Nope. We checked with missing persons, of course. She isn't listed as missing. At least, not yet. How old do you think she is?"

"My best guess is around thirty-five. And, before you ask – no, she wasn't sexually assaulted. However, she was pregnant. Probably four to five months."

"Ah, crap," Wickers moaned. "Two lives lost and probably for some no-good dumb-ass reason. What else, Donna?"

"I think she fought her attacker. I got a few scrapings from under the nails. We're checking it out. Maybe, we'll get lucky. However, being in the water could have destroyed any other evidence that was on her body."

"Hopefully not. She wasn't in the water that long. Maybe you'll get something we can use.

"I wouldn't count on it, Ralph. I'm about to take x-rays of her teeth. I'll send you a copy. Most likely sometime this afternoon."

"Thanks, Donna." Chief Wickers walked over to the door. "Donna," he said.

She turned and looked at him. "Yes?"

"Are you seeing anyone right now?"

Donna grinned. "Why, Ralph, what would your wife say?"

Wickers laughed. "Probably tell me to get lost, as she kicked my ass out of the house."

"Why do you ask?"

Wickers hesitated a second. "Well, I guess it wouldn't make any difference if you were seeing someone. It's just that Ida's brother is in town and, if you're not busy Saturday night, I was wondering if you'd like to join the three of us for dinner. It's not like a date. I think he feels like a third wheel, and if you were there, he might…"

"I'd love to join you," Donna interrupted. "Send me the details. Now, get out of here. I've got work to do."

Wickers smiled. "Great. I'll text you."

"Wonderful," Donna exclaimed. "Now, out!"

Alex glanced over at his brother and frowned. "What's this all about, Mike? What did you do now?"

"Shut up, dork face. I didn't do nothing."

"Then what's going on?"

"How should I know?"

"Why else would mom and dad want to talk serious to us?"

"I said I ..." Mike stopped talking and looked up as Jack and Maggie walked into the room.

"Boys, your mom and I ..."

"I didn't do anything wrong," Alex interrupted.

"Me either," Michael said.

Maggie smiled. "Settle down, boys. Your father and I just want to ask you a couple of questions. You aren't in trouble."

"I don't know, Mags," Jack added. "They look like they could be guilty to me. Maybe they did do it."

"Jack, stop it. That's not funny."

"Sorry." He sat down across from the two boys and smiled. "I just want to mention that a woman was found dead in the lake. I understand it was an accident, and I don't want you to be concerned about it."

"Uh-huh," Michael said shaking his head. "I heard about it."

"Me, too," Alex declared.

"Well, the thing is, the police haven't been able to identify her. So, they are going from house to house and asking people if they saw anything strange on Sunday or Monday."

"What do you mean by strange?" Alex asked.

"You know. Cars you didn't recognize or people hanging around? I'm not sure, Alex. I guess anything out of the usual. Is there anything you remember? Weren't you guys out on the lake fishing on Sunday?"

"Maybe she belongs to that naked club," Alex volunteered.

"The police already checked that out. She didn't belong to it, but that was a good suggestion," Maggie said.

"Maybe she came from the body farm," Michael stated.

"No, they checked that, too."

"I can't think of anything," Michael said. "Some cars went by a few times, but with all the trees it's hard to see the road. We didn't see anything while we were fishing. Did we, Alex?" He shrugged. "Sorry, I can't help."

"Me, too," Alex said. "I don't know nothing."

"Anything, Alex," Maggie corrected.

"Sorry. I don't know anything."

"Well, if you think of something, let us know."

"Can we go now?" Alex asked.

"Run along, but don't go too far," Maggie told him. "Lunch is in half an hour."

"Wait a minute," Jack said. "One more thing."

"What?" Alex asked.

"If the police decide to talk to you guys, just tell them you don't know anything about it. Okay?"

"Okay, Dad," Alex said. "Can we go now?"

"Mike?" Jack said, staring at him. "Understand?"

"What could I tell him? Just like you said, Dad, I don't know anything and I didn't see anything," Michael told him, staring back at him.

"That was a good lunch, wasn't it, Mike?"

"It was okay," Michael replied, walking away from Alex.

"Where are you going, Mike?"

"I need to put gas in my bike."

"Again? You sure go through a lot of gas. Are you sure you don't have a leak?"

"I don't know. I guess I'll check," Mike replied as the two boys walked to the shed where the bikes were kept.

"How come you told mom and dad that I was fishing with you?" Alex asked.

Michael didn't say anything.

"Mike?"

Michael shrugged. "I don't know. I guess I figured it would sound better if they thought the two of us were together."

"What difference does it make? I don't get it."

"You know why, Alex."

Alex stared at his brother for a moment, then made a face as what Mike was saying sunk in. "You really are a pervert, aren't you? You were watching those naked people, weren't you? God, Mikey, what the hell is wrong with you?"

"What's wrong with me? There's nothing wrong with me. You're the one that's not normal."

"Why? Because I don't like to look at some dumb old naked women?"

"They aren't all old, Alex. Some are young like me."

"Where are you going?" Michael asked as Alex turned and started to walk back to the house.

"What do you care?"

"You better not tell mom and dad," Michael threatened.

"So, what if I do? Whattaya gonna do about it?"

"You better not or I'll tell them that you're gay."

Alex turned and looked at his brother. "What did you say?"

"I'll tell them that you like boys."

Alex let out a scream as he rushed toward his brother, hitting him full force with his body and knocking him down. "You take that back!" he yelled.

Michael looked up at him. "Or what? You gonna fight me?"

Alex stood there looking down at his brother, tears gathering in his eyes. "You know what? Screw you, Michael," he said as he turned and walked back to the house.

Chapter Ten

"I've got good news and bad news," Jack said, smiling. He took a sip of coffee, frowned, and set the cup down. "Does the coffee seem hotter to you lately?" he asked Maggie.

Maggie gave him an inquiring look and shrugged. "I don't know. Hotter than what?"

"Than usual. I think the machine is broken."

"It's working just fine, Jack. I haven't noticed any difference."

"Well, I do. I'm going to have it checked out."

Maggie frowned. "What's going on with you this morning?"

"I paid almost two grand for that damn machine and I expect it to work," he exclaimed.

"Jack, you said something about good news and bad news. Remember?"

"Oh, right." He smiled. "Sorry. I got distracted. Which would you like first?"

"I don't know. I guess the bad news."

"Nope. The good news first," Jack replied.

"Oh, for God's sake, will you get on with it?"

"The property next door is for sale. I put a bid on it and it looks like it's going to be accepted. If it is, our property will go east as far as Yellow Snake Road. No more surprise neighbors for us."

"That is good news." Maggie gave him a pensive look. "And ..."

"Ah, yes. The bad news. It seems that the nudist camp is holding its own financially and the owner has no desire to sell."

"Shit!" Maggie mumbled under her breath.

"It doesn't make a profit but the income does cover the expenses for running the place.

"I see."

"However..." Jack continued.

"What?"

"It seems that the owner of the camp has overextended himself on several other business ventures and is in some trouble."

"So, up the offer," Maggie told him.

"I haven't made an offer. I wanted to test the waters before putting my big toe in it. In fact, the owner, Wesley Saunders, doesn't know anything about me."

"You had Nelson inquire, didn't you?"

"Yep. And, he did an excellent job of checking Saunders out. He is underinsured. If something should happen to that place ..."

"Like a tornado or perhaps a fire," Maggie interrupted, smiling.

"Well, yes. God forbid. But the insurance would never cover replacing the buildings and he certainly couldn't afford it out of his own pocket. So, I think we should be patient and see what happens."

"I want that place gone, Jack."

"I know. However, unless there is an act of God, I don't think that is going to happen anytime soon. I'm sorry, Maggie."

"Doesn't have to be an act of God, does it? Oh, well. I guess we'll just have to learn to live with it being there, won't we?" She smiled at him. "Can I make you some breakfast? How about some bacon and eggs?"

"You understand, Mags? It's not for sale."

"Of course, I understand. I heard you. The nudist camp isn't for sale. Now, do you want breakfast or not?"

"Maggie?"

"Yes, dear. What is it?"

"I know that look. What are you thinking?"

"School starts pretty soon. It's going to be strange not having the boys here all the time."

"I know. But it will be good for them. It's about time they found a few new friends."

"I know. I just can't believe how big they are getting. Especially, Mike. He's almost as tall as you," Maggie said.

"He's strong, too. It's going to take a lot for Alex to fill Mike's shoes."

"We shouldn't compare them, Jack. They are their own persons."

"I know. This move has been good for them."

"For us, too," Maggie said. "By the way, when was the last time the gas tank was filled? The boys have been using a lot of gas in their bikes and I can't remember when Skully last filled it."

"I'll check it out. I've been thinking of getting a larger tank. It seems like we are constantly having this one filled."

"That might be a good idea. How much bigger?"

"It varies, but I'm thinking one that will hold at least a couple of hundred gallons."

"That seems excessive," Maggie told him.

"Not really. I'm still doing the research. We'll see."

"So, you'll check when it was last filled, then?"

"Yes, Maggie. I'll check it out. Now, how about that breakfast?"

"Coming up."

"Are the boys up?"

"Mike is. I think he's swimming. Alex is sleeping in."

Jack walked over to the kitchen window and looked out the window. "I don't see Mike. He's not in the pool."

"Well, he was a little while ago. Why don't you go wake Alex? It's time he was up. I swear that boy would sleep his life away if he could."

"Ah, let the boy sleep."

"Please, Jack. It's almost eleven."

Jack sighed as he pushed his chair away from the table and stood up. "All right, I go wake him."

Maggie grinned. "I'm sorry you have such a hard life, Jack."

"He's not in his room," Jack told her a few minutes later, as he entered the kitchen.

"Is he showering?"

"No. He's not up there. He must have gone out." He looked at the table. "Is breakfast ready?"

"You've been gone for two minutes. I'm not a witch, you know. I can't just wiggle my nose and your food suddenly appears in front of you. Give me a break, Jack."

"Geez. I'm sorry. Let's just skip it, shall we? It's almost lunchtime. Why don't I round up the boys and we drive into town for lunch?"

"I'm sorry. I didn't mean to be bitchy. Are you sure you don't want something now?" Maggie asked smiling.

"Actually, I like that place we went to last time. Let's go there again."

"You mean The Meat and Eat Diner?"

"Yeah, that's it. You liked it, didn't you?" Jack asked her.

"I did. But how about we try a different place?"

"That's fine. Whatever you want," Jack replied.

"Will you call the boys and I'll go change?"

"That's a plan." Jack walked over to her, bent down, and kissed her. "I love you, you know."

"I know. I love you, too."

"Michael, this is dad. Respond, please." Jack checked the walkie-talkie to make sure it was on. "Mike? Come back, Mike." He waited for a moment. "Mike, are you there?" He turned as Maggie walked up behind him.

"What's the problem?" she asked.

"Neither one of the boys is responding," Jack told her.

"Try again. Sometimes they leave the walkie-talkies on their bikes when they go wandering off."

"Dad?"

"Did, you hear that?" Maggie asked.

"Barely. I think it was Mike." He flipped a switch and yelled, "Are you there, Mike?"

"You don't have to yell. I can hear you. What's up?"

"We're going for lunch. I want you boys back here."

"I'll be right there. Did you let Alex know?" Mike asked his dad.

"Isn't he with you?"

"No. I don't know where he is. He was gone before I got up this morning."

"Well, come on in. I'll keep trying to reach him."

He glanced over at Maggie, who looked worried. "Don't start imagining all kinds of things, Maggie. He's probably just out of range or maybe his batteries died."

"Try his phone," Maggie instructed. "God, Jack, if anything ..."

"Just hold on, will you?" He rang Alex's phone and waited. "Nothing. It went straight to voice mail."

"Oh, God, Jack," Maggie cried out. "Something's happened. I know it. I can feel it."

"Please, Maggie, we don't know that. Let's wait for Mike and see what he has to say. He must have seen him if they were both in the woods. Or, at least, heard his bike."

"That's not necessarily so. You know that."

"He could have gone fishing. The reception is bad on the lake."

"Then, I'll kick his ass," Maggie replied. "He knows he's not allowed on the lake by himself."

"Mike should be here in a few minutes. Let's go back inside the house. We can decide what to do when he gets here."

"I don't know, Jack."

"Come on. It'll be okay."

Maggie stared at the woods, trying not to cry.

"Mags? Come on, honey?"

Maggie turned to him as tears filled her eyes. "I'm coming."

Chapter Eleven

Maggie got off her dirt bike and waited for Jack to pull up alongside her. He pulled his helmet off and shook his head, puzzled that they hadn't found Alex anywhere on the property. A few moments later Michael drove out of the woods and stopped by his parents.

"Where else could he be?" Maggie asked, more to herself than Jack or Michael.

"What, Mom? Michael asked her.

"Nothing. Just thinking out loud." She glanced over at Jack, wondering what was going on in his mind. "What now, Jack? What do we do now?"

"We covered a lot of ground. If he was out there, I'm pretty sure he would have heard our yelling or our bikes. I think we should call the police."

"No. He's got to be okay. Let's just wait a little longer. He'll come riding in and we'll all yell at him for being so stupid and everything ..."

"I'm calling Dan. It's going to be dark soon and we need help."

"What do you think, Mike," Maggie asked her son.

"It's not up to him," Jack exclaimed. "And, we need to eat something. It's after three and we haven't eaten all day. We need to keep our energy up, Maggie. It may be a long night."

"You think something horrible has happened, don't you?" she yelled.

"Right now, I'm not thinking one way or the other. But I know we need help." He walked towards the house.

"I'm calling Dan. How about you make a few sandwiches?"

"How can you even think about eating at a time like this?" she shouted.

"Come on, Mom," Michael said quietly, taking his mother's hand. "I'll help you make the sandwiches while dad calls Dan."

"I'm sorry I yelled. It's just that I'm really worried about Alex."

"We all are," Michael told her. "But we need to stay calm. Okay, Mom?"

"Okay." She glanced at Jack. "I'm sorry, Jack."

"Nothing to be sorry about. Let's go in. I need food."

"And, I need a bathroom break," Michael added, as he ran towards the house.

"What time did he leave the house?" Deputy Downing asked Jack.

"I have no idea. He was gone before any of us were up. We didn't know he was missing until around noon when we couldn't raise him on his phone or the walkies."

"And, you didn't hear him leave the house either?" Chief Wickers asked Michael.

"No. I was sleeping. I'm usually up before Alex. He likes to sleep late."

"You're sure he took his dirt bike?" Wickers asked.

"Of course. He never goes anywhere without it," Maggie said.

"Where do you keep the bikes?" Wickers inquired.

"We usually lock them in the shed." Jack hesitated a moment. "Well, Maggie and I make sure we lock ours up. Alex is pretty good at putting his away, too. But Mike has a memory lapse every so often and leaves his in the yard. Don't you, Mike?"

Mike looked away, not answering his father.

"And, you're sure his bike isn't locked in the shed?" Deputy Downing asked.

Maggie looked at Jack. "You checked the shed, didn't you?"

Jack closed his eyes and sighed. "I never even thought that it might be here." He stood up and headed for the front door. "I'll go check it out."

"Wait a second, Jack. I'll go with you," Dan said.

"How worried should I be, Chief?" Maggie asked as she watched her husband and Deputy Downing go out the door.

"I'm not sure. Has Alex ever done anything like this before? You know, disappeared for a day or two."

"You mean run away? Of course, not. He's a good boy, Chief Wickers. He rarely gives us any trouble."

"Well, I think we need to get some men out here to start searching the woods. I'm going to have Dan start checking with the neighbors to see if anyone has seen Alex today." He looked over at the door as Jack and Dan came back into the house. "Well?"

"His bike isn't in the shed," Deputy Downing said.

"Jack, is it possible that Alex took the boat out on the lake?"

Jack shrugged. "He has strict orders not to go out on the lake alone."

"But, is there a possibility?"

"Anything is possible," Jack told him. "But it wouldn't be like him." He looked at Michael. "Did you notice if the boat was gone?"

69

"I didn't check the boathouse, Dad. Didn't you or mom?"

"I didn't," Maggie said. "Jack? What about you?"

"Damn! What is wrong with me? That should have been the first place I checked. I'll go check it out."

"Dan, go with him. Maybe Alex took the boat and ran out of gas. He could be floating around on that lake hoping someone will see him. In the meanwhile, I'm going to call for a search party to be ready if we need them." He looked at Dan. "Go! Call me immediately if you find the boat."

"Would you like some coffee, Chief?" Maggie asked.

"No, thanks. If you don't mind, I'm going to step into the kitchen to make a call."

"That's fine." She looked over at Michael. "Are you okay, Mike? You're very quiet," Maggie asked.

Michael glanced at her, shaking his head no. "What if something happened to Alex, Mom? What if he's hurt or something?"

Maggie got off her chair and walked over to Michael. "He's going to be fine, sweetie," she told him as she sat down and took his hand. "He'll be fine."

"But what if he isn't? What if this is all my fault?"

"Don't be silly. How could it be your fault?"

"We had a fight yesterday and Alex was really mad at me. Maybe he …"

"What did you fight about?" Maggie interrupted.

"I don't know. It was just a dumb argument and he got mad."

"Michael, what did you fight about?"

"I called him a pussy or something like that and he hit me." Michael grinned. "Actually, he knocked me down. I didn't think he had it in him."

70

"Did you hit him back?"

"Of course not. He ran into the house, all upset. That was the last time he talked to me and now he's gone. So, it's my fault, isn't it?"

"Oh, honey, of course, it isn't your fault. You and Alex fight all the time. He wouldn't disappear just because you called him a name. You know that." Maggie put her arms around Michael and hugged him. "Now, you stop thinking like that." She glanced up as Chief Wickers walked into the living room. "How did it go?"

"We're getting a search party set up right now. They're on standby if we need them."

"Good."

"Would you mind if I check out Alex's room, Maggie?

"What for?"

"I just want to take a look, if that's okay with you."

"It's fine. Mike, will you show Chief Wickers where Alex's room is?"

"Sure, Mom."

"Hold on," Wickers said, as he glanced at his phone. "That's Dan calling." He listened for a moment and frowned. "All right. Come on back to the house." He ended the call and looked at Maggie. "The boat is missing."

Chapter Twelve

"How long has he been gone?" Fred Sullivan asked Deputy Downing.

"Since early this morning. We've got a bunch of guys from town coming out to search the woods."

"You don't say? Well, I'd like to join in, but these old knees of mine aren't what they used to be."

"No problem, Fred. Just keep an eye open and let us know if you see him or anything out of the usual."

"Will do, Deputy. That's a nice family. I sure hope you find him safe and sound," Sullivan told him.

"We all do, Fred."

Deputy Downing got in his squad car, drove down Twisted Tree Road, turned left on Yellow Snake Road, and headed for the nudist camp. He sighed as he turned into the entrance to the camp, wishing he was any place but here. He drove to the main building and parked his car. As he exited his car, he noticed Mandy walking out of the front door of the building, naked as a jaybird.

"Well, hello there, Deputy," she called out as she headed towards his vehicle. "What can I do for you?"

"Mandy," Downing said, acknowledging her. "How are you?"

"As you can see, I'm just as good as can be."

"I wonder if you saw a young boy around here today. Alex Keegan seems to be missing. He decided to go off this morning without telling anyone where he was going. His parents are pretty worried about him."

72

"Are you talking about one of those boys that live in that big house on Twisted Tree Road?"

"I am. He's about twelve or thirteen years old. He rides his bike out in the woods a lot."

"Oh, yes, those dirt bikes. They are noisy things, aren't they? Does he have an older brother, maybe fifteen or sixteen?"

"He sure does. Have you seen him?"

"I've seen the two of them fishing out on the lake sometimes."

"That would be them. So, have you seen the younger boy today?"

"Nah, He stays away from here. Now, his older brother – well, that's another story."

"What do you mean?"

"His brother likes to look, if you get my drift. He thinks we don't see him hiding in the bushes, but we know he's there. He's not hurting anything, so we just ignore him. Sometimes, when he's out in his boat, he gets pretty close to shore and anchors the boat and just sits there and watches us through his binoculars."

Deputy Downing shook his head and sighed. "I'm sorry about that. I'll give him a warning when I see him."

"Oh, please don't do that. He's just curious, that's all," Mandy replied. "Most boys are at that age. It's not like he's doing anything wrong, Deputy, and I don't want to get him into trouble."

"Did you happen to see the boat today, Mandy?"

She thought for a moment. "I didn't, but I wasn't swimming today. However, there were quite a few members on the beach. Why don't I check with them and see if anyone saw anything? I'll give you a call and let you know what I find out."

"Do you stay here at night?" he asked her.

"I do. Red wants someone here all the time in case of any problems, so I'm here almost every night. I work long hours during the season. Red lives about ninety minutes away in Rock Garden and he goes home almost every night."

"Was he here today?"

"He was. He left about thirty minutes ago. He should be here in the morning if you want to talk to him."

"I'll do that. In the meanwhile, please check with your people and see if they know anything. Mr. and Mrs. Keegan are pretty upset."

"I'll do that," Mandy said, smiling. "By the way, Deputy, if you're ever bored, why don't you stop by some night? We could have a drink or two and get to know each other a little better."

"Maybe, I'll do that. Thanks for the invitation. And, my name is Dan," Downing responded, as he opened up the car door and got in.

"Dan, it is," Mandy commented, waving as she turned and walked away.

Dan took a few moments to look her over as she walked towards the lake. *God, she's gorgeous. I don't think I've ever met anyone who is as comfortable with their body as she is*, he thought, as he started the car and drove away.

"Who is it?" Pete asked, speaking into the intercom.

"Sorry to bother you. This is Deputy Dan Downing. I would like to speak with Dr. Simmons."

"One moment."

Downing closed his eyes and smiled, remembering how Mandy looked while they had their conversation.

"Come on down, Deputy," Pete said, as the gate swung open.

Downing drove the short distance to the office and parked his car. He glanced over at the building and saw Dr. Simmons walk out the door and head towards him. As he got out of his car he called out, "Dr. Simmons. Good to see you again."

"What can I do for you, Deputy?" she asked.

"One of the Keegan boys has gone missing," he told her. "I was wondering if you or your people happened to see him at any time today."

"The Keegan boy. That would be the family that lives south of us, I believe."

"That's right. The younger boy can't be found and we're checking with everyone to inquire if they know anything."

"Well, I certainly haven't seen him. I doubt anyone else here has either. We talk a lot, so if a strange boy was seen wandering around someone would have said something."

"I didn't think he'd be around here, but we have to cover all the bases, you know. His parents are quite concerned."

"As they should be. I knew when that family moved in that something bad was going to happen," Dr. Simmons stated.

"What do you mean – something bad?"

"When you leave two young boys loose on dirt bikes riding wildly around in the woods and allow them to drive like maniacs in a boat on a lake, something is bound to go wrong. Don't you agree, Deputy?"

"I wasn't aware that they were causing a problem. However, right now our concern is finding Alex. Would you please check to see if anyone here saw him today? It would be greatly appreciated."

"I can do that. Most of them are in town having dinner. As soon as they get back, I'll check it out and get back to you. Do you have a number where I can reach you?"

Downing pulled out a card and handed it to her. "You can reach me at this number. Day or night. You can call any time," he told her.

"I'll do that if I hear anything. Good evening, Deputy." She grabbed the card, turned, and walked away.

Downing watched her enter the building and shook his head. "Man, she's abrupt. Maybe she should take a few lessons from Mandy," he said softly, grinning.

Deputy Downing parked his car and looked around. He counted fourteen cars, plus the sheriff's vehicle outside the Keegan house. A group of men had gathered on the edge of the woods and Chief Wickers was giving them instructions regarding the search. Downing was about to get out of his squad car when his mobile rang. He didn't recognize the caller ID. "Downing here," he answered.

"Dan, this is Mandy from the nature club."

Downing suddenly felt warm, excited that she had called him. "Hi, Mandy."

"Have you found the boy yet?"

"No, not yet."

"I've contacted everyone here and one of the men sunbathing on the beach this morning thinks he might have seen something unusual. He's not sure if it's anything that will help, but I thought I should let you know."

76

"Yes, of course. You did the right thing. You never know when the slightest thing can lead to something helpful. So, what did he tell you?"

"He's pretty sure he saw a boat out on the lake around nine or nine-thirty. It had to be Keegan's boat, as no one was using ours at that time and I'm not sure if the body farm even has one. I've never seen one if they do."

"It had to be Alex. It looks like we better get someone out on the lake looking for that boat."

"Well, that's the thing. He's not sure there was anyone in the boat when he saw it. And, Dan, we found the boat. It's close to the shore between our property and the body farm. It's half-filled with water and it's resting on the bottom of the lake."

"Did you find Alex? Was he in the boat?"

"No. The boat was empty when we found it. We looked but we didn't touch anything. You know, so we wouldn't disturb any evidence of anything."

"That's good, Mandy."

"Another thing that seems strange is that there are holes in the bottom of the boat. They are quite large and we could easily see them. It looks like that boat was sunk on purpose. At least, to me it does."

"Okay. Now, do me a favor and keep everyone away from the boat. Someone will be over to check it out in a few minutes."

"Would that be you?" she asked softly.

Downing grinned. "I'll talk to you soon."

Chief Wickers frowned as Deputy Downing repeated the conversation that he had had with Mandy. "Damn!" he exclaimed. "I was hoping it wouldn't come to this."

"We're gonna have to call in divers, aren't we?" Downing asked.

"We are. I'll make the call. They'll have to bring in a couple of boats. The nudist camp has a boat launch, don't they?"

"They do. In fact, it's the only place where you can launch a boat on this whole lake."

"We will set up over there. Will you call ... What's her name, again?"

"Mandy."

"Right. I want to drive over and take a look at the boat. You said you can get to it from the shore, didn't you?"

"Yeah. It's close to the beach."

"Okay, then. I'll let her know that we'll have divers and boats coming in the morning. But first I'm going to talk to the Keegans and update them." He sighed. "God, I hate this part of the job," exclaimed.

"Do you think he's dead?" Downing asked softly.

"Who the hell knows?

"Should I join the search party?"

"No. You stay here. I might need you."

"Do you still want me to call Mandy?"

"What? Oh, that. Yeah. Give her a call and let her know I'm coming over, will you? Perhaps you could mention that it would be a good idea if she put some clothes on."

"Hell, no."

"What do you mean no?"

"I would never ask her to do that. She should never put clothes on, as far as I'm concerned."

Chief Wickers stared at him for a moment and suddenly grinned. "My God, boy, I think you're in love."

"You would be, too, if you weren't married. She's positively gorgeous. And, she's so nice, Chief."

"Did you ask her if she's married?"

"Well, I didn't think – I mean she doesn't act – hell, I don't know."

"You don't know if you asked her?"

"Well, no, but I don't think she is."

Wickers shook his head and chuckled. "Then, I suggest that until you find out, you go ahead and look all you want, Dan, but keep it at that." He waited for a reply. "Dan, did you hear me?" he finally asked.

"I heard you," Downing replied.

"I mean it. We don't know if anyone at that nudist camp is involved in this. For now, you keep it professional. Got it?"

"Yes, Sir. I got it."

Chapter Thirteen

"How long have you been up?" Jack asked as he walked into the kitchen, rubbing his eyes.

"I haven't been to bed," Maggie replied, taking a sip of coffee. "I don't know how you can sleep with Alex missing."

"I nodded off a few times, Mags, but believe me I haven't had a whole lot of sleep."

"Then, how come you didn't know I wasn't in the bed with you?" She looked away. "Oh, just never mind. It's not important." She walked over to the sink and looked out of the window. "It's almost light. They'll be starting their search pretty soon."

"I know," Jack replied, glancing at the coffee pot. "Would you mind putting on another pot of coffee? I'm going to get dressed and head over to the nudist camp. I'd like to take a thermos of coffee with me."

"Chief Wickers asked that we stay here, Jack. He made it plain that he doesn't want us there."

"Well, Chief Wickers can kiss my you know what. It's my kid that's missing, not his. I'm going."

Maggie stared at him for a moment. "Then, I'm going, too."

"I'd rather you stay here with Mike, Maggie. I need you here in case of a phone call or ..." Jack turned away from her and started sobbing.

"Oh, Jack," Maggie cried out as she walked over to him and put her arms around him.

"I'm so afraid, Mags," he said between the sobs. "What if something horrible has happened to Alex?"

"We have to be positive, Jack. You can't think like this. They are gonna find him and he's gonna be fine. You'll see."

Jack stepped back and looked at her. "How I wish I could believe that," he exclaimed, wiping the tears away with the palm of his hand. "But I think we both know that probably isn't the case."

"I can't give up hope. I just can't."

"I'm sorry. I'm going to get dressed." He turned and walked out of the kitchen.

Maggie waited until he was out of sight before she sat down at the table, put her head down on her arms, and wept.

Sheriff Wickers stood on the shore watching the boats search the lake. The county had managed to send three boats and six divers, who would alternate their time in the water. The sonar equipment they were using had been a great help in shortening the search time and the success rate in finding bodies. He sighed as one of the boats cut its motor and stopped. A diver appeared out of the water holding up his arm, meaning he had found something.

"Did they find something?"

Wickers jumped and turned to see who had scared him. "For God's sake, Jack, you scared the crap out of me. How long have you been standing there?"

"Not long. They found something, didn't they?"

"I'm not sure." His radio crackled and he responded. "Wickers here."

"We got something, Chief."

81

"Hold up a minute. Jack, I want you out of here. I asked you not to come this morning."

"I'm not going anywhere. Just ask if they found Alex, will you."

"Are you there, Chief?" a voice asked.

"What have you got, Milo?"

"We found a dirt bike."

"Say again."

"A dirt bike. We found a dirt bike."

Jack grabbed Wickers' arm. "Ask him what color it is,"

"Could you tell the color?"

"It's blue."

Jack's face turned white and he struggled not to fall to his knees. Wickers grabbed his arm and kept him from falling. "I told you to stay home." He motioned to one of his police officers to come over.

"You need me, Chief?" the young officer asked as he approached the two men.

"I want you to put Mr. Keegan in a car and take him home. And, stay with him. I don't want him back here. Understand?"

"Yes, Sir."

"Good."

"I'm not leaving," Jack shouted.

"Yes, you are. Officer, please take Mr. Keegan home."

By eight-thirty in the evening, the search party had packed up its gear and left. The entire lake had been searched, and except for the boat, the bike, and some old junk lying on the bottom of the lake, nothing else had been found. Chief Wickers was confident that Alex was not in the lake.

"But his bike was in there," Maggie exclaimed. "You have to look again."

"Maggie, the search party covered every inch of that lake. He's not there. The bike was found fairly close to the shoreline and I think someone revved it up and let it go straight into the water. That, along with the holes in the boat makes me think that someone is trying to make us believe that Alex drowned. If he did, his body isn't there. We need to keep looking."

"So, he may still be alive," she murmured. "But, where?" She looked over at Jack. "Where would he go, Jack?"

Jack shrugged. "I have no idea," he told her. "Your guess is as good as mine."

"Do you think he might have gone to Chicago?"

"God no. Why would he go there?" Jack asked her.

"I don't know. To see old friends maybe. I'm just trying to make some sense of this."

Chief Wickers looked surprised. "I thought you moved here from St. Paul."

"Alex has friends that moved to Chicago. They always talked about seeing each other, so it was just a thought." She glanced over at Jack. "Sorry. That was crazy. He would never do that. Right, Jack?"

"Yeah, I guess," he said, looking uncomfortable. "God, I'm so tired I can't think straight. I need some sleep."

Chief Wickers pushed his coffee cup away and stood up. "I'll leave you guys to it, then. Get some rest."

"What happens tomorrow, Chief," Maggie asked.

"We're bringing in some dogs and we'll finish searching the woods. We'll be going through those woods next to you, too."

"I recently bought that land."

He sighed. "I heard that. Anyway, I'm sorry we weren't more successful today, but not finding Alex is a good thing."

"He's been gone two days, Chief. Even I know that the more time that goes by the chances of finding him alive get slimmer," Jack declared.

"Jack!" Maggie yelled. "Don't say that. You can't think like that."

"She's right," Wickers told him. "We haven't given up yet. We may still find him safe and sound. Good night folks. I'll see you tomorrow."

Jack watched out of the window until he saw Wickers drive off. He turned and stared at Maggie. "What the hell were you thinking?"

"I'm sorry. It just slipped out."

"That slip may have started a whole bunch of trouble, Maggie."

"I'm sorry."

"Sorry doesn't cut it. You better pray that Wickers forgets you said that." Jack opened the front door and walked outside.

"Where are you going?" Maggie called out.

"I need to cool off before I do something stupid."

"Can I come with you?"

Jack turned and stared at her. "No, you may not. What's wrong with you anyway? Just go to bed, Maggie."

"I'm so so sorry," she said softly, tears running down her cheeks.

"Mom, is everything okay?"

Maggie turned and smiled. "Everything is fine, Mikey. I'm tired, that's all. It's been a long day."

"Were you and dad fighting?"

"Not really. I said something stupid and he's upset with me. He'll get over it."

"Aren't you going to bed?"

"I thought I'd wait for your dad to come back."

"I think it would be better if you went to bed. You're worn out. You can talk to him in the morning. Come on, Mom. Go upstairs and go to bed."

Maggie looked at her son and smiled. "You're right." She took his hand as the two walked to the stairs. "I'm so lucky to have you," she told him, squeezing his hand.

Chapter Fourteen

"They've completed the northwest side of the property," Deputy Downing told Wickers. "The dogs went crazy when they got near the body farm."

"We expected that to happen," Wickers said. "That's why we went over that area twice. What now?"

"They're almost finished searching the north section. When they finish that they'll check out the woods on the west side. I don't know, Chief. It isn't looking good."

"I know. But we have to be thorough."

"I understand Jack Keegan just bought that section west of him."

"He did. He owns a lot of property. It must be nice to have so much money."

"What did he do before he moved here?" Downing asked.

"He was a janitor. A very lucky janitor who won a huge lottery."

"That's right," Downing said. "I think he said something about that."

"I'm gonna drive back to the station," Wickers informed Downing. "I've got a few things that need tending to."

"Will you be back out?" Downing asked.

"Yeah, but it may be a few hours."

"Oh, wait. Did I mention that the people at the nudist camp are searching their woods? Do you remember Red?"

86

"Yes, I know who Red is. I'm still trying to get the picture of him sitting there naked out of my head."

Downing grinned. "It was quite a sight, wasn't it? Anyway, Red got everyone together and they decided to search on their own. They don't have a lot of wooded areas, so if there is anything there, they should be able to find it."

"That's nice of them," Wickers stated. "I hope they are wearing shoes."

Deputy Downing grinned. "They are. Everyone is dressed. Even Red. It's kind of weird."

"What's that?"

"Seeing them with clothes on. Mandy looks quite sexy dressed."

Wickers smiled. "I thought she looked quite sexy undressed."

"Oh, she does. That goes way beyond sexy."

"You better behave yourself, Dan."

"I know. You have no worries there, Chief."

"Good. I'll see you later."

"Rory, I want you to check out the Keegans," Chief Wickers told him as he walked into the Police Station

Officer Rory Canty glanced up from his desk and looked at Chief Wickers. "For what?"

"Everything you can find. Financials, employment history, criminal background, where they lived before moving here, whatever. You know the routine."

"What's the deal?"

"They have a kid missing. I need to check them out."

"Still didn't find him, huh?" Canty asked.

"Nope. I'll get his details and a recent picture from his parents. If we don't find him today, we'll need to enter his info in The National Crime Information Center."

"What about posters?"

"Yeah, we'll do that, too."

"Do you think he's a runner?" Canty asked.

"Not really. All the evidence points to foul play."

Canty stared at Wickers for a moment. "You think he was murdered?"

"I sure as hell hope not, but it's looking that way to me." He glanced over at the coffee pot, decided against any more coffee, and headed towards the door.

"Are you leaving?" Canty asked.

"I've got a dentist's appointment. It shouldn't take that long. After that, I'll be back out at the Keegan house. Only interrupt me if they find the boy. I'll check in with you when I leave the dentist."

"Ten-four," Canty called out, as the Chief closed the door.

"We're calling it," Wickers yelled over to Downing. "Tell the men to come in."

"We still have an hour or so of daylight," Downing called out as he walked towards Wickers.

"They've covered it all, Dan. Some of it more than once. Let's face it. He's not here."

"Come in, guys," Downing yelled into his radio. "Search is over. Come on in." He glanced over at Chief Wickers. "Damn shame. Where do you think he is?"

"I haven't a clue. I figured we'd find him in the lake for sure."

Wickers and Downing stood in Keegan's yard watching the search party walk out of the woods. After a few minutes, most of the men were standing around talking to each other.

"Where are Curt and Dick?" Downing asked one of the men.

"They were a little north of us with the dogs. They should be here in a few minutes."

"Here they come now," Downing declared. "I can hear the dogs barking."

"God those dogs are loud." Wickers waited until the two men and their dogs appeared. "Can I have your attention?" he yelled waving his arm in the air.

Downing let out a sharp high-pitched whistle to get the men's attention. "Okay, guys. Quiet down. Chief Wickers wants to talk to you," he yelled.

Wickers waited a few seconds before he spoke. "I want to thank you all for your time. I know you give up a lot when you go out on these searches. Most of the time we get lucky, but unfortunately, yesterday and today didn't get us the results we were looking for. We've covered the entire area. Hell, some of it twice, and I'm confident that Alex is not here." He turned and looked at the Keegans, who were standing just outside of their front door listening. "We're sorry, Jack and Maggie. Trust me, we're not done looking for Alex. Hopefully, we will find him safe and be able to bring him home to you." He glanced over at Downing. "You want to finish it up, Dan?"

"Just one more thing. Each of you will be getting a voucher for a dinner for you and your family at Wilkerson's Family Restaurant. You can pick the vouchers up at the police station. Remember! This is for you and your immediate family. No uncles or aunts or grandmas and grandpas."

Downing waited until the laughing ended. "That's it, men. Thanks again for your help. Curt and Dick, thanks for bringing in the dogs. You'll be getting a bag of dog food for your trouble. Just let Officer Canty know what kind they eat and we'll drop a bag of food off at your house." He glanced over at Chief Wickers. "Anything, else, Chief?"

Wickers shook his head no. "Drive safe, everyone." He walked over to where the Keegans were standing. "Can I talk to you for a few minutes?"

"Of course," Jack replied. "Come on in."

"Dan? You want to come in here when you're through there?" he yelled.

"Sure thing, Chief," Downing called out. "Be right there."

"I'm sorry," Maggie told Chief Wickers, as she blew her nose again. "I can't stop crying." She pulled another tissue from its box and wiped the tears away from her cheeks.

"Nothing to be sorry for, Maggie," Deputy Downing said.

"We're sorry we didn't find Alex," Wickers said. "But you have to look at this as a positive thing. There's a good possibility that Alex is alive. He may have run away."

"No way!" Maggie exclaimed. "Alex would never do that."

"We have to consider it." He glanced over at Jack. "You've had some time to think about this. Can you think of any reason Alex would leave?"

Jack shook his head no. "I've racked my brain trying to figure out why he would do such a thing, Chief. I can't come up with anything."

Wickers glanced around the room. "Where is Michael?"

"Upstairs," Maggie told him.

"Would you ask him to come down here, please?"

"I'd rather not," Maggie replied. "He's taking this hard. I don't want to upset him any more than he already is."

"I'm sorry, but I need to talk to him. There are a few questions I want to ask him and you need to be present when I do. I'd rather do it here than down at the station."

"I don't understand," Maggie said, looking bewildered. "What are you saying, Chief?"

"I need to talk to him, that's all. I understand he's upset but we're running out of time here, Maggie. He may know something ..."

"If he knew something, he would have told us," Jack said interrupting Wickers.

"Dan, would you go ask Michael to come down here?" Wickers asked.

"Never mind, I'll get him," Jack said angrily.

"Thank you."

"Michael, I want you to think real hard now. Can you think of any reason why Alex would run off?"

Michael looked down at his hands and shook his head no.

"Michael, look at me," Wickers said.

Michael glanced over at Wickers, looking like he was about to cry.

"I want you to tell me about the fight you and Alex had on Tuesday."

"What fight?" Jack asked.

"It was nothing," Maggie told him. "He already told me about it."

"Why did you fight, Michael?" Wickers asked again.

"It was nothing," Michael said. He looked away for a moment. "Well, it wasn't anything to make him take off, that's for sure," he told Wickers.

"Tell me anyway."

"He was upset because I told mom and dad that we were together fishing on the lake when that lady was found dead."

"That was a lie?" Chief Wickers asked him.

"Yeah. Alex wasn't with me. I was fishing by myself."

"You know you're not supposed to go off and leave Alex alone, Mike," Jack shouted.

"Please, Jack. I'd appreciate it if you didn't interrupt."

"Sorry," Jack told Wickers.

"Does this happen a lot? You leaving Alex while you go off fishing?"

Michael shrugged. "Sometimes. He doesn't like fishing, so he just rides around on his bike while I'm out on the lake."

"Do you catch a lot of fish?" Deputy Downing asked.

Chief Wickers looked over at him, wondering what Downing was getting at.

"A few. I usually throw them back in."

"What else do you do while you're out on the lake?" Downing asked.

Michael looked away, not answering Downing.

"I know you watch the nudists, Michael. You sit in your boat with your binoculars and spy on them, don't you? And, sometimes you hide in the bushes and watch them."

"No!" Michael yelled.

"I know you do. The people at that camp are well aware that you watch them."

"I'm not a perv."

"Is that what Alex calls you? A perv?"

"No." Michael looked at Maggie. "Mom, I'm not."

"Did he call you that, Michael?" Wickers asked. "Did he call you a perv because you like to watch naked people?"

"He was going to tell on me," Michael blurted out. "He was going to tell mom and dad that he wasn't with me."

"So, what's the big deal? Why lie?" Wickers inquired.

"I wasn't supposed to leave him alone in the woods. I didn't want to get in trouble. We fought and he called me a perv."

"Excuse me, Chief Wickers," Jack chimed in. "Mike, we've all joked about that before. He didn't mean anything, so why did you get so upset?"

"I was afraid he would tell you that I look ..." He turned away, ashamed.

"I told you it was bad for the boys to be so close to that place," Maggie yelled at Jack. "I was right, wasn't I?"

"I don't look at the men," Michael exclaimed defensively. "Only women. I'm not gay."

"All right, everyone. Calm down," Wickers said. He glanced over at Michael. "No one is calling you gay. What else, Michael?"

"Nothing," Michael said adamantly.

"Michael, what else happened with Alex?"

"I told him that he wasn't normal because he didn't like to look at naked women. I said I was going to tell mom and dad that he was gay." He looked at Jack and Maggie, tears rolling down his cheeks. "I'm sorry. I didn't mean it. It was a dumb fight, that's all. He pushed me and ran into the house."

"Did you hit him?" Jack asked.

"No. I swear, I didn't."

Chief Wickers sat back in his chair and stared at Michael. "That's it? Nothing else happened?" he asked after a few moments.

"That's it. I swear."

"Do you have any idea how Alex's bike wound up in the water?"

"No, Sir."

"Or, why the boat was sunk?"

"No," Michael said shaking his head.

"Are you sure there isn't anything else you want to tell me?"

Michael shook his head no.

"All right, then. Come on, Dan. We've got work to do."

"That's it?" Jack inquired.

"For now. However, let me say this. I don't believe Alex ran off somewhere. We'll do everything we can to find him, but I wouldn't get my hopes up if I were you. The bike and the boat in the water don't make sense if he ran off."

"You think he's dead," Maggie declared.

"I think it's a good possibility," Wickers replied.

Chapter Fifteen

"I thought this was your day off, Rory," Chief Wickers stated as he walked into the police station.

"It is, but I wanted to stop by for a minute and talk to you."

"It couldn't wait until tomorrow?"

"Probably, but I thought you'd like to know what I found out about the Keegan family."

"It must be good for you to come in on your day off," Wickers said.

"You tell me. Did you know that Jack Keegan died twelve years ago?"

Wickers sat back in his chair and stared at Canty. "Is that right? He looks pretty good for a dead person."

Officer Canty grinned. "At least that's what his death certificate says. And, guess what?"

"What?"

"He has no relatives that I could find."

Wickers poured himself a cup of coffee, walked over to his desk, and sat down. "I see."

"Well, aren't you surprised?"

"I am and I'm not. I've had a feeling that something was off with that guy. I just couldn't put my finger on it."

"Do you think that they're hiding from something?"

"You think? Did you find anything on Maggie or the boys?"

"Near as I can tell, Alex and Michael are their children. According to their birth certificates, both of them were born in Chicago. I couldn't find anything on Maggie at all. Absolutely nothing."

"Did you check out Margaret Keegan? Maggie could be a nickname."

"I checked everything I could think of."

"She must have a social security number. She worked as a teacher, didn't she?"

"I found nothing on her. The way I figure it Keegan isn't Jack's real name. He has been using a dead man's social security number. I couldn't find any record of them being married either."

"What about tax returns?" Wickers inquired.

"Nope. Plus, if they've ever lived in St. Paul, I couldn't find any record of it."

"So, he's been Jack Keegan for twelve years. I wonder who the hell he was before that."

"And, who the heck is she?" Officer Canty added.

"It looks like we need to do a little more digging," Wickers told him.

"Like where? I've checked out everything I can think of."

Wickers shook his head. "I don't know. Let me think on this for a while."

"Aren't you going to ask the Keegans about this?"

"Not yet, Rory. I want to see what else I can find out first."

"Well, something is fishy."

"Have you run his fingerprints?" Wickers asked.

"I did and I got a hit for Jack Keegan. They match the prints we took when Alex went missing."

"This makes no sense whatsoever. Are you sure about all this, Rory?"

"I'll double-check it if you want. I doubt anything is going to change, though."

"Do it tomorrow. It's your day off and you should get some rest."

"I guess," Canty replied. He scratched his chin. "Well, I guess I should go. The little woman will have breakfast ready and I haven't even shaved yet." He glanced back at Wickers as he started to leave. "Why not?"

"Why not what?" Wickers asked.

"Why can't you ask them? You might get an answer. The least they can do is deny it."

Wickers grinned. "Maybe I will. In the meanwhile, I'll do some more digging. By the way, Rory, I wouldn't be calling your wife the little woman if I were you."

"Why not?"

"Does she still have that temper?"

Canty smiled. "Hell, yes."

"Think about it."

Canty looked puzzled for a moment, then grinned. "Right. I see what you mean. Thanks. Have you heard anything about our lady in the lake?" he asked Wickers.

Wickers shook his head no. "We still haven't heard anything. Her prints are being run, her dental records are being checked, and, so far, no one has reported her missing. Right now, it's a dead end."

"Someone has to know something," Canty said.

"Well, if they do, they're not talking."

"Do you want to drive into town and get some breakfast?" Jack asked Maggie.

She glanced up and stared at him. "How can you eat?"

"I'm hungry and I'm not going to let myself go to pieces because our son is missing. And, you shouldn't either, Mags. I'm sure Mike is hungry. How about it? Let's go get something to eat."

"Why don't you and Mike go? I'm not in the mood and I'm not hungry."

"Fine. Where's Mike?"

"He's out in the yard."

"He's not riding his bike, is he?"

"No. He's just sitting by the pool."

"What's he doing?"

"I don't know, Jack. Probably thinking about how much he misses Alex."

"I'll see you later," Jack told her as he opened the front door to leave.

"Are you actually going to leave me here all alone?" Maggie called out.

"Do you want to come along?"

"No."

"Then I'll see you later," he said, closing the door behind him.

Maggie stared at the closed door. "Bastard," she mumbled and started to cry.

"Hey, Jack," Chief Wickers said, surprised to see Jack and Michael in the restaurant. "Just the two of you today."

"Maggie didn't feel up to coming along. Mike and I decided we wanted breakfast and we didn't want to have to cook it ourselves. Right, Mike?"

Mike looked up from his plate. "That's right," he told Wickers as he shoved a fork full of pancakes in his mouth.

"Well, it looks like you're enjoying the food," Wickers said.

"I'll say," Jack agreed. "This is the best breakfast I've had in ages."

"How's Maggie holding up?"

Jack shrugged. "As expected, I guess."

Chief Wickers looked around the restaurant and waved "There's Ida."

"Your wife?" Jack asked.

"Right. We thought we'd enjoy a meal together. We haven't seen much of each other the past few days."

"Sorry about that," Jack told him.

"No. I didn't mean it like that. It's just that I spend more time being a cop than a husband. I don't know how she puts up with me. I'll see you later." He started to walk over to his table, hesitated, and turned back to Jack. "Are you going to be home later today?"

"Yeah. We don't have any plans. Why?"

"I might drop by later."

Chapter Sixteen

"Anything else you need, Dr. Simmons?" Jason, the groundskeeper at the FBI Body Farm, asked.

Dr. Simmons looked up at him and smiled. "I think we're good for the rest of the day, Jason. Why don't you take the rest of the day and spend some time with your family?"

"They ain't here. They left."

"Are they off visiting relatives again?"

"No. I mean they left for good."

"Oh, Jason. I'm so sorry. What happened?"

"Damn wife just left with the kids. I come home and find a note telling me not to try to find them. Bitch cleaned out my checking account, too."

"When did this happen?"

"Last Tuesday, it was. I won't miss her but I'll miss my boys. Can she do that, Doc? You know just take my kids and money and run off?

"I'm not sure, but I'd sure ask Chief Wickers if I were you."

"I can't do that. He won't help me none," Jason replied, looking uncomfortable. "He don't like me."

"Why in the world would you say that he doesn't like you?"

Jason shrugged. "I don't know."

"Come on, Jason. You can tell me."

"We've had a few run-ins, that's all. He's got it in for me."

"I doubt that's true. You really should talk to him and see if there is anything the police can do about your situation."

"Just forget it," Jason said, getting agitated.

"What did you do to make you think he doesn't like you?"

"I said forget it," Jason yelled. "It's none of your business."

"Please don't yell at me, Jason. I'm just trying to help," Dr. Simmons said.

"You're no different, you know?" Jason told her angrily. "You women are all alike."

"Excuse me. I think that's enough. I'd like you to leave before this gets out of hand and you do something you'll regret."

"So, what are you gonna do? Fire me?" he asked, glaring at her.

They glanced over as the door opened and Chad walked in. "Am I interrupting?" he asked.

"Not at all. Jason was just leaving. Isn't that right, Jason?"

Jason gave her a dirty look, turned, and walked towards the door.

"Jason. Wait!" Dr. Simmons called out.

Jason turned and looked at her. "What?"

"I understand that you're going through a bad time right now and you're angry. However, I'm not your enemy, Jason. You've worked here for a long time and I'd hate to see you leave for good. So, take a day or two and pull yourself together. If you decide you don't want to continue working here, let me know. However, if you want to keep your job here, I'd be happy to see you come back. But, with a better attitude. Understood?"

"Understood," Jason said shaking his head yes. "I'm sorry. I guess all this has been building and I took it out on you."

"So, you'll be back?"

"Yes, ma'am. I'll be back tomorrow."

"Good. I'll see you then."

"What was that all about?" Chad asked.

"His wife took his kids, cleaned out his checking account, and left him. He's upset and needed someone to take it out on. I guess that was me."

"That's gotta be rough going through something like that. Although, I ..."

"What?"

"Well, doesn't he seem a little strange to you? I mean, he's not a very friendly guy. He rarely talks to any of us except you."

"And, that's only when he has to. I know he's a little off or maybe different is a better word. But he does a decent job here and I'd hate like hell to have to break in someone new."

"So, what else is going on?" Chad asked, trying to change the subject.

"I need to make a phone call, Chad. Would you mind?"

"You mean leave?"

"Clever boy. Yes, leave."

"I'd like to speak to Chief Wickers, please," Dr. Simmons said.

"Sorry. He's not in right now. Can I help you?"

"Will he be in today?"

"I expect him back soon. Can I have him give you a call?"

"Would you ask him to call Dr. Simmons?"

"Can I tell him what it's about?"

"I just have a question for him, that's all."

"I'll give him the message. Oh, wait. He just came in. Hold on a minute."

"Thank you."

"Dr. Simmons, how are you this morning?"

"I'm fine. How about you?"

"I'm good. How can I help you?"

"Chief Wickers, I was wondering if you could do me a favor. I have an employee working here and he's made a few comments that I'm concerned about."

"An employee? That has to be Jason Setzman. Right?"

"How'd you know that?"

"Well, unless you've hired someone else, I believe Jason is the only person working there who isn't affiliated with the FBI."

"I don't know if you're aware that Jason's wife left him. She took off with his money and the kids. He's extremely upset, which is understandable. While we were having a conversation about this, he commented that you don't like him."

"Well, I wouldn't go so far as to say that," Wickers said a little defensively.

"Well, there must be a reason for him to say that. Which is the reason for my call."

"I'm not sure what you're getting at, doctor."

"We did a background check when we hired him and there was nothing that would set off any alarms. So, has anything ..."

"Dr. Simmons, let me make this easy for you. We have made frequent visits to the Setzman house over the past year. He has a fast temper and fast fists. So far, Mrs. Setzman has been the only recipient of those fists, but we've been concerned about the kids. Mrs. Setzman has refused to press charges against her husband. If she's left town, good for her."

"I see. So, he's a drinker then?"

"No. That's the thing. He doesn't drink and as far as we know, he doesn't do drugs. He just has a short fuse and blows up over the smallest things. I'm not sure how mentally stable he is."

"Do I have anything to be concerned about with him working here?"

"Have you ever seen him lose it?"

"Today is the first time. He wasn't violent but I'm not sure what may have happened if we hadn't been interrupted. What do you suggest I do?"

"I can't tell you what to do. I can tell you that if I were you and he was around all the time, I'd walk a fine line. I wouldn't want to get him upset."

"But he has no record. Right? You've never arrested him?"

"Nope. And, it's not because I didn't want to. I'm just glad his wife and kids are out of his reach."

"Thank you. I appreciate your candor."

"I hope this helped," Wickers said.

"Oh, it did. Thanks, again. Goodbye, Chief."

"Bye, Dr. Simmons."

Susan L. Paré

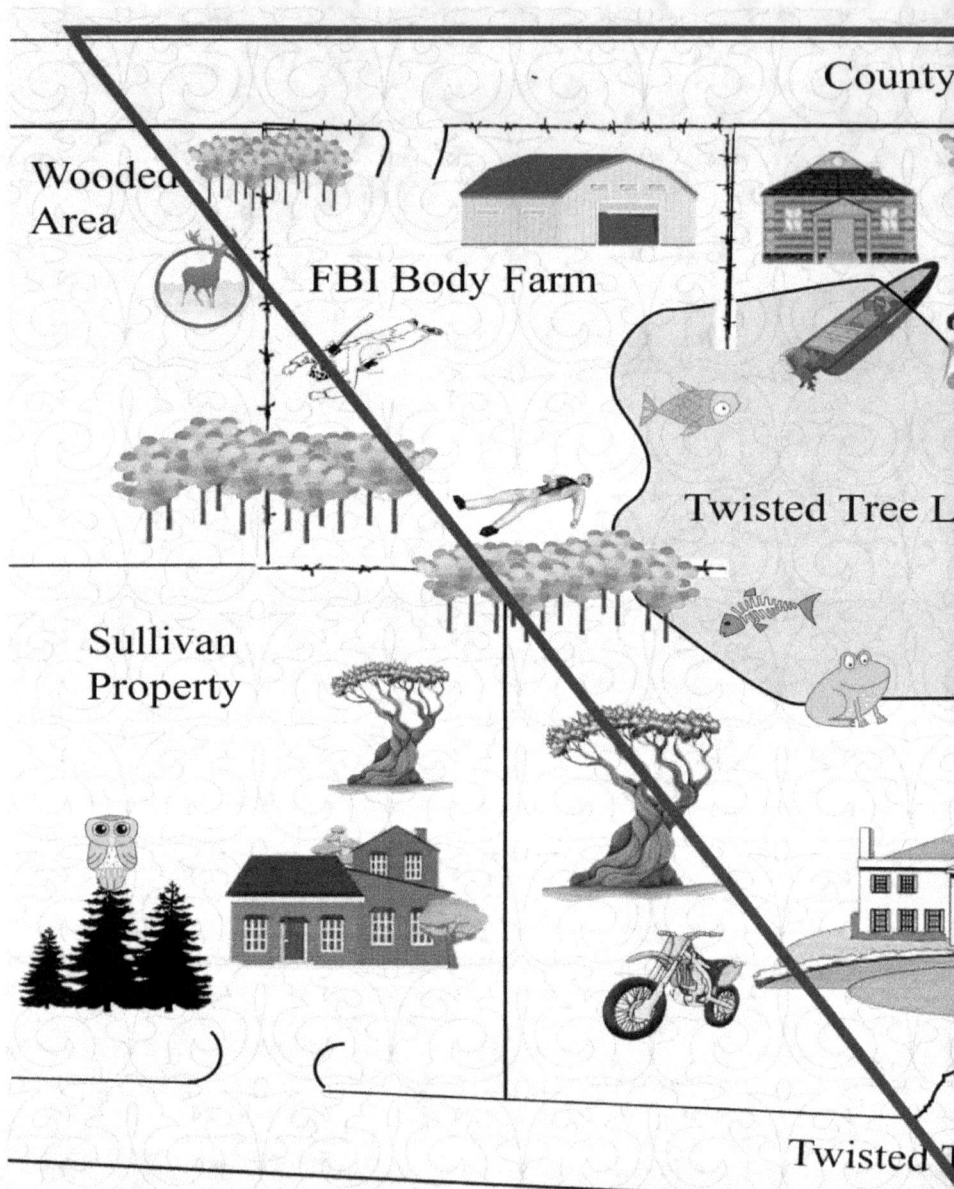

County

Wooded
Area

FBI Body Farm

Twisted Tree L

Sullivan
Property

Twisted

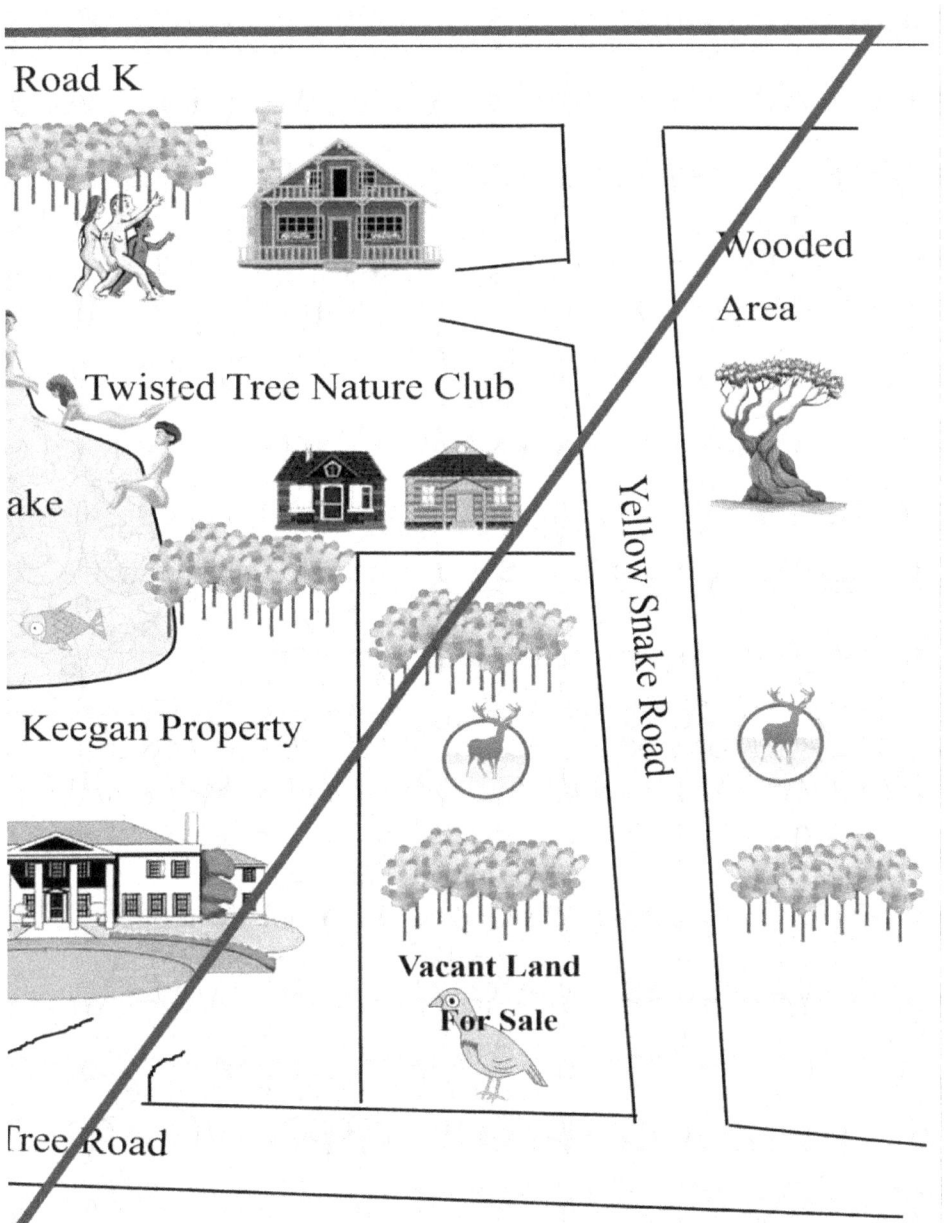

Road K

Twisted Tree Nature Club

Wooded Area

ake

Yellow Snake Road

Keegan Property

Vacant Land For Sale

Tree Road

Chapter Seventeen

"I don't care what you say. I'm not going to school here."

"Well, I'm sorry, Mike, but you don't have much of a choice," Maggie said.

"I hate it here. Why can't we move back to Chicago? I liked it there and all my friends are there and now that Alex is ..." He turned away from his parents, trying to hold back his tears.

"Mike, I'm sorry, but it's not an option. We are not moving to Chicago. You have to start school. It's the law, you know."

"Why can't I go live with Bud?"

"Because you can't. I know this is rough, but you need to give the school here a try. You'll meet new friends and you'll get into sports again. It won't be that horrible, Mike," Jack told him.

"It's not the same without Alex," Michael wiped his eyes. "It's all my fault he's dead, you know," he stated.

"Don't say that," Maggie exclaimed. "We don't know if he's dead and it's certainly not your fault."

"If he's not dead, then, where is he? It's been two weeks already. If he just ran away, he would be back by now. If I hadn't fought with him, he'd never have gone into the woods alone. It's all my fault." Michael turned and ran out of the room.

"What are we going to do?" Maggie asked Jack. "I don't know what to tell him."

"We need to get away for a while. Maybe a trip will take his mind off all of this," Jack suggested.

Maggie stared at him. "You can't be serious. We can't leave now."

Jack closed his eyes and sighed. "I don't know how to help him, Maggie. I can't even help myself. I feel like everything is closing in and I don't know what to do."

Maggie walked over to him, put her arms around him, and hugged him. "I wish there was some magic word I could say and everything would be back like it was. But there isn't and I can't fix it, Jack. I can't help you or Mike or …" She broke down, sobbing on his shoulder.

"I've got an idea," Michael exclaimed, as he walked back into the room. He looked at his parents. "Sorry."

Maggie turned and tried to smile. "It's all right. What's your idea?"

"Why don't you guys home school me? You don't do anything all day. You've got the time."

Jack looked at Maggie and grinned. "Just what makes you think that your mother and I are smart enough to teach you anything?"

Michael hesitated a moment. "Yeah, you're right. I don't know what I was thinking. You're definitely not smart enough," he answered, grinning.

Jack grabbed his arm and pulled him close to Maggie and himself, hugging him. "You're a little smart ass. You know that?"

"Just kidding, Dad."

"What do you think, Mags? Should we try that home school thing?"

"Are you serious, Mike? Is this what you want?" she asked.

"For now, maybe. I can always go back to school, but I just don't want to go now. I need a little more time."

"We could try it for a semester and see how it goes," Jack declared. "What do you think, Mags?"

"School starts in a few days so, if we are going to do this, we better get moving and find out what we need to do."

"I want to take Mandy out. Is it okay or are we still investigating the people at the club?"

Wickers tried his best to hold back a grin. "No, it's not okay."

"Why not? There's nobody there that did anything wrong."

"We have two ongoing investigations, Dan. You know that. Until we find out who killed our Jane Doe and what happened to Alex Keegan, I want you to keep your distance from her."

"Nobody there did anything wrong. You just don't want me going out with her because she's hot and you're jealous."

Wickers laughed. "You think I'm jealous?"

"Of course. Mandy is hotter than any woman that lives in this town."

"So, you're saying you think she's hotter than Ida?"

Downing bit his lip to keep from smiling. "Ida is okay, I guess. I'm sure she was pretty hot stuff back in her day, but now she's old like you. Don't get me wrong. She's held her own pretty good and she's still a good-looking woman. But Mandy – well, she's absolutely gorgeous. Without a doubt, she's positively the most stunning magnificently beautiful woman I've ever seen," he told Wickers, trying to keep a straight face.

"You think I'm old?" Wickers asked him.

"Hell, yes. What are you now? Forty-five? That's old, man."

"I can still take you, you smart-mouthed pup."

Downing laughed. "I doubt it, but I'm not gonna give you the chance to find out. I'm afraid I'd hurt you."

"You have a call, Chief," Canty called out to Wickers, interrupting their bantering.

"Who is it?"

Canty shrugged. "I don't know. They asked for the guy in charge."

"Find out who it is," Wickers told him. He waited for a moment.

"It's about a car he thinks has been abandoned."

Wickers grabbed his phone. "Chief Wickers here. What's this about a car?"

He listened for a moment, shook his head agreeing with the caller, grabbed a pen, and started taking notes. "I see. No, you did the right thing. About how far down the road would you say?"

He made a notation on his pad. "I'll meet you there in half an hour. What did you say your name was? Got it." He hung up the phone.

"What was that all about?" Downing asked him.

"That was a Denny Tuttle. He says he lives out past Old Quarry Road. A car has been parked on the side of the road for a few weeks now. He figured he should tell us about it."

"I know a Vince Tuttle," Canty commented. "I wonder if they are related."

"I don't know. I've never heard of any Tuttles that live around here. I'm gonna take a drive out there. You wanna come along?" he asked Downing.

"I guess."

"It will take you more than half an hour to get there," Canty told him. "Old Quarry Road is at least a forty-five-minute drive."

"Whatever. Let's go take a look. He said it has an Illinois license plate on it. Perhaps it's connected to our Jane Doe."

The plates don't go with the car," Chief Wickers told Deputy Downing. "They were reported stolen about two weeks ago."

"What about the car? Who does it belong to?"

"The VIN is being checked. We should get that information before long. In the meanwhile, get a tow truck out here and get this car back to town."

"There's a suitcase on the back seat," Downing mentioned. "Should I take a look inside?"

"No, don't touch anything. We'll go through it after we get it back to the station."

"Do you think it belongs to our Jane Doe?" Downing asked him. "If this car has been here for two weeks, the timeline is right."

"I'm not jumping to any conclusions, Dan. We need to see what we're dealing with first."

"But it could belong to her. Right?"

"It probably is her car. Call Gobert's Towing and tell them we need a vehicle towed.

"I'm on it," Downing said. "Don't you think we should check the trunk first? Who knows what could be in there?"

"After we get it back to town," Wickers replied.

"Okay, let's get that trunk open, "Wickers told Officer Canty.

Canty placed the crowbar under the lid of the trunk and pushed. "Damn," he exclaimed when the trunk didn't open.

"Give it a little more muscle, Rory," Wickers said.

Canty moved the crowbar over a little more towards the center of the lid and pushed again. Suddenly, the trunk sprung open. "There, that did it," Canty declared.

"Holy crap, what a mess" Downing exclaimed. "Hey, Chief, look at this," Downing yelled across the garage.

"Whatcha find?" Wickers asked.

"A picture. You aren't gonna believe this."

Chief Wickers walked over to his deputy and looked at a picture that Downing was holding. "Hold on, I need to glove up." He stared at it. "What the hell?" he said looking at the picture. "Is that who I think it is?"

"I'm pretty sure," Downing told him.

"What else is in there?"

"There are some clothes and stuff and… wait, here is a letter addressed to a Sophia Regio," he said as he held up an envelope.

"Let me see it," Wickers said.

"It's got a Chicago address," Downing said, as he handed the letter to Wickers. "There's no return address on the envelope."

Wickers carefully removed a sheet of paper from the envelope and opened it. "There's no signature."

"What does the letter say?"

"One warning is all you get. Stay away or you'll be sorry."

"What the hell is that supposed to mean?" Downing asked.

"I imagine just what it says."

"Do you think that's Jack Keegan in that picture?"

"It sure as hell looks a lot like him. Maybe he has a twin," Wickers replied.

"Sir?" Officer Canty called out.

"What is it?"

"There are proof of insurance cards in the glove box. The name on the cards is Sophia Regio."

Chief Wickers sighed. "Well, it looks like our lady finally has a name. Let me have those, will you, Rory?"

Rory walked over to Wickers and handed him the papers.

"Thanks. All right, you guys. See what else you can find. I've got a few calls to make."

"Are the addresses the same?" Downing asked.

"What?"

"The addresses. Are they the same? You know, the one on the insurance card and the one on the envelope?"

Wickers glanced at the insurance card and shook his head yes. "It's a match."

Chapter Eighteen

"I want you to run a check on Jason Setzman."

"What for?" Canty asked Wickers.

"See if he was in any trouble before he moved here. He's got a bad temper and him and I have had more than one run-in. I wonder if he had anything to do with Alex."

"You think he killed the Keegan boy?"

"I'm not saying that, but maybe the Keegan kid got on the FBI property somehow and had a run-in with Setzman. It's possible and it could have gotten out of hand."

"Do you think he had something to do with the woman in the lake, too?"

Wickers shook his head no. "I don't think so. The Keegan kid maybe, but I'm pretty sure he didn't do the woman we found. I think that might have something to do with Jack Keegan."

Canty looked surprised. "What makes you think that?"

"A few things that aren't adding up and my gut."

"I'll check Setzman out."

"Dr. Simmons."

"Hello, Doctor. This is Chief Wickers. I'm following up on our last conversation. I was wondering if Jason Setzman is still working there or did you let him go?"

"Jason is still working for me. We had a nice conversation and I agreed to keep him on as long as there aren't any more outbursts. He's been fine so far."

"I'm glad to hear it. Please feel free to call me if any problems arise."

"I will. Thank you for checking," Simmons replied.

Chief Wickers hung up the phone and sat back in his chair. "Crap," he muttered.

"What's wrong?" Canty asked.

"I'm not looking forward to the next few phone calls."

"Are they about the Jane Doe?"

"Yeah, except I don't think she's a Jane Doe anymore."

Wickers picked up the phone and dialed the number of the insurance agent that was listed on Sophia Regio's insurance card. "Yes, hello," he said after a few moments. "I'd like to speak to Patrick Duffy, please." He waited for a moment. "Mr. Duffy, this is Police Chief Ralph Wickers from Prairieville, South Dakota. I'm calling regarding an incident that happened here a few weeks ago. I was wondering if you have a client named Sophia Regio?"

He made a few notes as Duffy replied. "What kind of a car does she drive, Mr. Duffy?"

"I believe it's a 2018 Toyota Camry," Duffy told him. "What's this about, Chief Wickers?"

"Could you give me a description of her?"

"Sophia is - let me check here on the computer. Ah, yes. She is 34 years old, has dark hair, brown eyes, and she's 5'6" tall."

"Do you know if she is married?"

"According to this, she's divorced. What's going on, Chief Wickers."

"I'm not really at liberty to say right now. We are trying to identify a body and there's a possibility it might be Ms. Regio."

"Oh, no. That's terrible. Do her parents know?"

"No, and I'd appreciate it if you didn't say anything to them. We're not sure it is Ms. Regio and until we can positively identify our Jane Doe, we don't want to talk to her parents. Do you understand, Mr. Duffy?"

"Absolutely. I won't say anything."

"Can you give me her current address?"

"Of course. It's 27234 George Street, Chicago."

"And, that's her current address?" Wickers asked.

"As far as I know."

"Thank you, Mr. Duffy. I appreciate your help."

"I have a picture of her. If you want, I could email it to you," Duffy told him.

"That would be a big help. I'd appreciate that. Thank you for your help. The email address here at the station is www.prairievillesdpolice.com."

"I'll send it off to you straight away. Bye."

"Well?" Deputy Downing asked as he handed Wickers the picture that he had printed out from the email sent by Duffy. "Same lady?"

"Same lady, Dan. It's her, for sure."

"What now?"

"What now? What do you think?"

"We go talk to Jack Keegan?" Downing replied.

"Exactly."

"But we aren't positive that's him in that picture, are we?"

Wickers sighed. "I guess not. But we can ask him, can't we?"

"Mom, did you ever find out about those trees?"

"What trees are you talking about, Mike?"

"Those trees that are all twisted. You know, the ones that Mr. Sullivan said are like that because of a tornado."

Maggie smiled. "Oh, those. Yes, I checked it out. A tornado didn't do that. They grew that way. Certain types of oak and aspen trees will twist as they grow. It's kind of rare, but it happens."

"So, it wasn't a tornado like Mr. Sullivan said."

"No, Mike, it wasn't."

"Then, why would he say that?"

"Probably some old tale that was passed down from one generation to another. I'm sure he believes it, so let's not say anything about it to him. Okay?"

"Okay," Michael replied.

"Do you know where your dad is?"

"He went outside."

"Would you go tell him dinner is ready?"

Jack watched as the squad car pulled into his driveway. He waited until Chief Wickers turned off the car before he approached. "Chief, how you doing? Hey, Dan. What's up," he inquired as Wickers and Downing got out of the car.

"Dad, dinner's ready," Michael yelled from the front porch."

"I'll be right there," Jack shouted back. He looked at Chief Wickers and smiled.

"We need to talk to you, Jack," Wickers said.

"Can it wait?" Jack asked. "We're about to sit down to dinner."

"No. I need to talk to you now. Is there a place inside where we can talk in private?"

Jacked stared at him, a perplexed look on his face. "What's this about? Dan, what's going on?"

"Is there?" Wickers asked again.

"We can talk in the study," Jack told him.

"Jack, your dinner is getting cold," Maggie exclaimed as the door opened and Jack walked in. "Oh, I didn't know ..."

"They have something they need to talk to me about," Jack interrupted. "You two go ahead and eat."

"Can't it wait until after you've eaten?" Maggie asked, obviously a little upset.

"Sorry, Maggie. It can't," Wickers told her.

"Well, what's so important it can't wait?"

"This way," Jack told Wickers and Downing, ignoring Maggie.

"Jack?" Maggie said.

"Later, Maggie. You and Mike eat. No sense in all of us having a cold meal."

"Please, sit."

Jack walked behind a large oak desk and sat down in an expensive leather chair. He watched as the two policemen sat down in chairs facing him.

"I have to say, all this mystery is starting to make me a little nervous," Jack said.

"We wanted to talk to you without Maggie being present. This might be embarrassing for you."

"For crying out loud, Chief, what is it?"

"Do you remember the woman we found in the lake a few weeks back?"

"Of course, I do. A person doesn't forget something like that, do they?"

"We're pretty sure we've identified her as Sophia Regio from Chicago. Does that name ring a bell, Jack?"

Jack thought for a moment and shook his head no. "Not that I can recall."

"Perhaps this will refresh your memory," Dan said handing Jack the picture found in Sophia's suitcase.

Jack stared at it for a few seconds. "Is that her?" he asked, looking at Wickers.

"It is. The bigger question is – is that you?"

Jack looked at the picture again and frowned. "It kinda looks like me, but it isn't. I've never seen this woman and there's no way that's me in that picture."

"Take another look, Jack," Wickers instructed. "Are you sure you don't know her?"

"Of course, I'm sure. Where did you get this from, anyway?"

"It was in a suitcase we found in her car."

"Well, I'm sorry, but I can't help you."

"Do you mind if we ask Maggie?"

"No, I don't want you asking Maggie. She doesn't know her either."

"If you're so sure of that, then why don't you want us to ask her?"

"Because she's had enough grief to last a lifetime. I don't need you adding to it."

"I'm sorry, but I think we're going to see if Maggie can help out." Wickers looked at Downing. "Will you go ask her to come in here, please, Dan? Jack, I'd like you to leave the room."

"No," Jack said adamantly. "This is my house and I'm staying right here."

"Then, I'll have to take you both down to the station and continue this conversation there."

Jack gave Wickers a dirty look. "Fine," he replied sarcastically. He stood up and walked out of the room, passing Maggie and Downing as they entered the den.

"What's going on, Jack," Maggie asked.

"It's all a bunch of bullshit, Mags."

"Would you take a seat, please?" Downing asked as he closed the door to the den.

"What's this all about," she asked, looking baffled. "Did Mike do something wrong?"

"This isn't about Michael," Downing told her.

Maggie's face turned white. "You've found Alex. Oh, dear God, don't tell me he's dead," she cried out, starting to cry.

"No, no," Wickers said. "This isn't about Alex."

She stared at him. "Then, what the hell is going on? Why would you scare me like that?"

"Let's start over," Wickers suggested. "Maggie, this is about the lady we found drowned in the lake a few weeks ago. We've managed to identify her and ..."

"It's about time," Maggie declared.

"Anyway, we were wondering if you knew her."

"Why would I know her?"

"Her name is Sophia Regio. Does that mean anything to you?" Wickers asked.

Maggie thought for a moment and shook her head no. "Regio? No, I don't recall ever meeting anyone by that name."

"Do you think Jack ever met her?"

"I can't recall that he ever mentioned that name," she told him, looking puzzled. "Why do you think he would know her?"

"We found a picture in her car," Wickers told her. "I want you to take a look at it." He handed her the picture, watching her expression closely.

"Is this Sophia?" she asked.

"It is," Dan said.

"I don't know her." She held out the picture to give it back to Wickers.

"Wait. Take a closer look."

Maggie stared at the picture again and shook her head. "What am I looking for?"

"Is the man in that picture Jack?"

"What are you talking..." She hesitated, looking confused. "It kinda looks like him, doesn't it? I mean, this could be his twin brother."

"That's what we said," Dan told her.

"But this isn't Jack," she said. "The nose – from what I can see of it – has a bump. Jack's doesn't. Plus, the hair is way too light. Jack's hair is a lot darker than this. This isn't Jack. Jack has never been this heavy, either." She handed the picture back to Wickers. "You're way off. I'm sure this isn't my Jack."

"You're sure?"

"Positive."

"All right. I guess we're done here," Wickers said. "Thanks for your help, Maggie."

"Where did you say you found this picture?"

"It was in her car. It had been abandoned not too far from here. So, I guess you can understand why we were sure that it was Jack. You know, with the car found not far from where her body was found on your property, plus the picture and – well, we had to ask, didn't we?" Wickers replied.

"Of course," Maggie said, smiling. "Have you heard anything regarding Alex?"

"I'm sorry, but no. And, believe me, you'll be the first to hear if we do."

"What do you think?" Deputy Downing asked as he got into the squad car. "Do you believe them?"

Chief Wickers shrugged. "I'd like to, but I'm pretty sure they recognized Sophia."

"Was she ever reported as missing?"

"Nope, and I'd like to know why. Duffy, from the insurance company, mentioned her parents. You'd think they'd know if she's missing, wouldn't you?"

"Maybe, she's not," Downing commented.

"What do you mean? It's been almost a month since we found her. They must have missed her by now."

"Not if she told them she was going to be gone for a while. Maybe she said she was going on vacation or something to do with work. There are all kinds of reasons her parents wouldn't think she was missing."

Wickers thought for a moment. "You're right, Dan. It's time I contacted the police in Chicago and ask them to let her parents know that she is dead. There's no question who she is and they should be told."

"Perhaps, they could ask them if she ever talked about Jack Keegan."

"Absolutely. We need to find out why she was here and how she got in that lake."

Chapter Nineteen

"Come on in," Dr. Simmons said.

"I'm sorry to bother you, Doctor, but I need to ask you a question."

"No bother. What is it, Jason?"

Jason Setzman looked uncomfortable. Ever since his blowup with the doctor, he had been walking on eggshells, afraid he'd say the wrong thing to her.

"It's all right, Jason. I'm not going to bite."

"Well, it's just that I was wondering if you got in another cadaver, that's all."

"Why would you ask that?" Simmons replied, looking perplexed. "I've always made you aware when we get a new shipment, you know that."

"Well, I found a shallow grave that I don't remember being there before."

"Where is it?" Simmons asked him, concerned about what he was telling her.

"Well, that's the thing. It's over in section seven and I don't remember any cadavers being there."

"There shouldn't be. How close to the fence?"

"Pretty close," Jason replied.

"How shallow is the grave? Can you see the cadaver?"

"Yes, ma'am. At least some of it."

"Let's go," she told him, as she stood up. "Show me, Jason."

"Yes, ma'am. I've got the Mule out front."

Jason watched as Dr. Simmons carefully brushed some of the leaves and dirt off of the body. He stared down at Simmons, who was looking a little queasy.

"Are you all right, ma'am?" Jason asked.

"I'm fine, Jason. I think this could be the Keegan boy," she said softly.

"The boy that went missing about a month ago?"

"Yes. Don't touch anything else, Jason. We need to call Chief Wickers and get him out here."

"We can call from here, can't we? I've got my cell phone."

"Let's go back. This is a crime scene now. And, Jason, please don't say anything to anyone before the police get here."

"God damn it!" Wickers exclaimed as he slammed the phone down.

Officer Canty jumped, surprised at Wicker's outburst. "What's wrong?"

"Shit!" Wickers turned away and walked over to a window and stared out. "Where's Dan?" he asked after a few moments.

"Getting donuts."

"Get him back here. Now!"

"Yes, Chief."

Wickers picked up the phone and dialed the County Coroner's Office. "Dr. Dempsey, please." He waited for her to pick up.

"Dr. Dempsey."

"Donna, this is Ralph. The body of a young boy has been found. I think it might be the Keegan boy.

"Where is he?"

"In a shallow grave at the FBI's Body Farm. I'm headed over there now. How long before you arrive?"

Chief Wickers and Deputy Downing stared down at the body, still partially covered with dirt and dried leaves. "I expected it to be worse, seeing the amount of time he's been missing.

"It's bad enough," Wickers replied. He turned to Dr. Simmons, who was standing a few feet behind him. "You said Jason found the body?"

"That's right."

"And, you call this area section seven. Is that right?"

"Yes, that's right," she replied.

"And, there are no other cadavers in this section?"

"That's correct. This is the furthest section from the main buildings. It also backs up to the fence, so we decided not to use this area for now."

Wickers turned as a vehicle approached the area. "That must be Dr. Dempsey." He watched as the doctor walked towards him.

"Ralph," she acknowledged him.

"Donna, you made good time."

"I gather that's the body?" she asked.

"Yes," Dr. Simmons told her. "We believe it could be the Keegan boy."

Dr. Dempsey walked over to the shallow grave, made the sign of the cross, and bent down. She carefully brushed the leaves and dirt away from the boy's face. "It's been about a month since he went missing, hasn't it?"

"That's correct," Wickers replied.

"The body is actually in better condition than I would expect for this time of year. Of course, the fact that it has been partially covered and the extensive shade from all these trees could explain that." She continued to examine the body, turning it for signs of foul play. She glanced up at Wickers. "Have you called for transportation?"

"They are on their way," he replied.

"I'd say that due to the amount of decomposition, the body has been here between three to five weeks. I'll be able to tell more when I get it back to the lab."

"Can you tell if it's a male?" Dr. Simmons inquired.

"It most likely is, but with this degree of decay I can't be sure without further examination." Dr. Dempsey looked at Wickers. "You said the boy that went missing was twelve?"

"That's right."

"This could be a twelve-year-old child," Dempsey declared. "It could also be a short adult." She looked at Dr. Simmons. "What do you think, Doctor? "You've probably seen more dead bodies than I ever will."

"I agree with you."

"Which is?" Dr. Dempsey asked.

"Wait and see."

Three hours after the body had been removed by the coroner, Jack Keegan barged into the police station reception area. "Where's Wickers," he yelled.

Officer Rory Canty jumped up from his desk and quickly blocked the doorway to the room where Wickers was sitting at his desk. "Hold it there, Sir," he demanded.

"Get out of my way. I want to talk to Wickers."

"It's okay, Rory," Wickers said softly, as he walked up behind Canty.

"Why the hell didn't you tell me that you found Alex?" Keegan shouted. "My boy is dead and you don't even have the courtesy to come and tell me?" He glared at Wickers. "What the hell kind of a person does that?" he asked, as tears filled his eyes. "Why didn't you ..."

"Easy, Jack," Wickers said. "We don't know for sure if it's Alex. We don't have a positive ID on the body we found."

"Who else could it be?" Jack asked as the tears rolled down his cheeks.

"Think about it. It's a body farm. There are bodies all over that place. It could be possible that an animal dragged a cadaver to the spot where the body was found. They are checking right now to be sure that all those cadavers are where they should be."

"But I heard it was a kid. It must be Alex," Jack said, wiping his nose with the back of his hand.

"It might be. But, until we are 100% sure – well, you'll just have to wait like the rest of us."

"You still could have come and told us," Jack muttered.

"That's not how we work. I'm sorry you found out about this. We try to keep these things quiet until we know something for sure."

"Maggie is a nervous wreck."

"I'm sure she is. I'm sure you are, too. I'm sorry but I have to ask you to be patient."

"How long before you know for sure?" Jack asked him, starting to calm down.

"It may take a few days. In the meanwhile, I suggest that you try to keep it together. Okay?"

Jack took a deep breath and let it out. "I'll try."

"Now go home. I'm sure Maggie and Michael need you there with them."

Chapter Twenty

"I'll be releasing Sophia Regio's body tomorrow," Dr. Dempsey told Chief Wickers. "Her parents are in town and have made the ID. It is Sophia."

"We already knew that," Wickers replied.

"And, now it's official. Have you talked to them, yet?"

"I'm meeting with them later this afternoon. I gather they've made arrangements to have her body sent back to Chicago."

"They have."

"We're keeping her vehicle in impound for now. I still haven't figured out why there was a stolen plate on her car."

"It doesn't make sense, does it?"

"How much do her parents know?" Wickers asked.

"Just what the Chicago police told them. That she was found in Twisted Tree Lake and that you are following up on a few leads. They didn't go into much detail. I guess they figured you can do that when you meet with them."

"Did her parents know she was missing?"

"No. It seems they didn't talk to her that often," Dempsey told him.

"I see. Anything else I should know?"

"They seem kind of odd to me, Ralph."

"In what way?"

"You'll see what I mean when you meet them. To me, they don't seem overly upset about her death. But, then, everyone handles these things differently. Maybe, I'm reading too much into it."

"I doubt it, Donna. You seem to read people pretty well."

"Call me after you talk to them. I'd like to get your opinion."

"I'll do that. Thanks. Oh, wait."

"What?"

"Anything on the body from the FBI Farm yet?"

"I haven't finished."

"Can you give me something?"

"It's a boy around twelve to fourteen years old. I'd say he died around a month ago. The clothes he was wearing match the clothes that Alex Keegan was wearing the day he disappeared."

"So, it is Alex," Wickers stated.

"Most likely, but I'm still waiting for the DNA report. I should have that by tomorrow."

"Thanks, Donna. I'll call you later."

"Mr. and Mrs. Romano are waiting in Conference Room One," Officer Canty said.

"We only have one conference room, Rory." Chief Wickers glanced at his watch. "It's only two-thirty. Our appointment is at three o'clock. How long have they been here?"

"About twenty minutes," Canty told him. "They know that they are early."

"Thanks, Rory." He opened the door to the conference room and walked in expecting to see a middle-aged couple. He hesitated for a moment, then held out his hand to Mr. Romano. "I'm sorry to meet you under these circumstances," Wickers told them. "You have my sincere condolences."

"Thank you," Angelo Romano replied. "This is my wife, Poppy," he said.

"Ma'am," Wickers said, as he shook her hand. "Sorry for your loss."

"Thanks," Poppy said. "She wasn't my kid, though. I'm – I was her step-mama. Isn't that right, Angelo?"

"That's right."

"May I ask if Sophia's mother is still living?"

"Nah, she kicked the bucket about ..." She looked at Angelo. "What is it now? About eight years?"

"Sophia's mother died twelve years ago from cancer," Angelo told Wickers. "Sophia was twenty-three at the time."

"Has it been that long, baby?" Poppy asked him.

"It has."

Poppy smiled. "That's right. I remember now. I was two years older than her when we got married."

"You still are," Angelo said.

"Are what?" Poppy asked, looking puzzled.

"Two years older than Sophia."

Poppy gave him a strange look. "Well, dah," she exclaimed after a few seconds.

Wickers picked up a pen and made some notes on a pad of paper. He looked up at the couple, wondering what Angelo had gotten himself into. Poppy seemed like a handful. "Mr. Ricci, were you ..."

"Please, call me Angelo."

"Of course. So, Angelo, did Sophia inform you that she was coming to Prairieville?"

"As I said, we didn't talk much. Since her divorce a few years ago, she pretty much stayed away."

"Was there a reason for that?" Wickers asked.

"Not really. We just seemed ..."

"Tell him, baby," Poppy blurted out.

"Poppy, please," Angelo said.

"I hated her, that's why!" Poppy practically shouted. "She was a real bitch."

"That's enough, Poppy," Angelo said softly. "We don't speak bad of the dead."

"Could you explain that?" Wickers asked.

"She was married to my brother," Poppy told him. "He was the nicest guy in the world and she broke his heart when she divorced him. Plus, she hated that I married Angelo. She didn't want him to be happy. She wanted him to sit in a chair and wither away and I made him happy. She hated that. Isn't that right, baby?"

"It seemed like it."

"I see. How long have you been married?"

Poppy grinned. "Tell him, Angelo. Do you even know?"

"Of course, I know. Poppy and I have been married for ten years."

"You remembered."

"Of course, sweetie. How could I forget that day?"

"Mr. Ricci – excuse me. I mean Angelo. When was the last time you saw your daughter?"

Angelo looked up at the ceiling, thinking. "I think it was two or three years ago."

Poppy punched Angelo on the arm. "No, you silly. It was a few months ago. Remember?"

Angelo shook his head yes. "That's right. When I ran into her at the market. But we only talked for a few minutes. I know she didn't mention taking a trip or anything. I would have remembered that."

"Nothing else?" Wickers asked.

"Not really. She said she might move but she wasn't sure. I told her to be sure to give me her new address if she did."

"You never told me that," Poppy said.

"Do you know if she was seeing anyone, Angelo?"

"You mean did she have a boyfriend?"

"She'd never find anyone as good as my brother," Poppy exclaimed. "He was the best thing and she threw it all away for some one-night stand."

"Please, Poppy. Just forget about it, will you? It's over." He glanced at Wickers. "She did mention that she had been seeing someone but that they had broken up because he moved."

"Did she give you a name?"

"No. As I said, we had drifted apart."

Chief Wickers sat back in his chair. "Well, I guess that's about it. If you do think of anything that might help us, please give me a call."

"I'll do that," Angelo replied.

"Can we go now?" Poppy asked as she unwrapped a stick of gum and shoved it into her mouth.

"One more thing before you go."

"Yes?"

"Did the coroner inform you that your daughter was pregnant, Mr. Ricci?

"What?" Poppy exclaimed.

"Are you sure?" Angelo asked Wickers.

"Yes. She was around four months pregnant."

"See, Angelo, I told you she was a little slut," Poppy said smugly.

Angelo turned and looked at her. "Shut the fuck up, Poppy. I don't want to hear another word out of your mouth."

Wickers stood up and walked towards the door. "If you wait here for just a moment, I'll have Officer Canty show you out."

"Nice meeting you," Poppy called out as Chief Wickers left the room.

Wickers sat down at his desk and called Dr. Donna Dempsey. "You could have given me more of a warning," he said when she answered the phone.

Dempsey laughed. "Are they a pair or what?"

"If I had married something like that, she'd be six feet under in the backyard."

"Well, there are a lot of older men who enjoy that type of woman."

"Seriously?" Wickers asked. "Why?"

"You need to ask?"

"I guess not."

"Did you find out anything?" Dempsey asked.

"Not really. She mentioned to her dad that she may be moving. Note, that he said may. And, that she had recently ended an affair because the man moved away."

"Jack Keegan?" she inquired.

"If that's him in that picture, it connects them. Other than that, we have nothing substantial to go on."

"I see. Well, I'm busy. I've got to go."

"Okay. Let me know when the DNA report comes in."

"You're the first one I'll call."

"Thanks, again, Donna."

Chapter Twenty-one

"Where have you been?"

Maggie gasped and put her hand over her heart. "You scared the crap out of me. What are you doing sitting here in the dark?"

"Where have you been, Mags?"

"I couldn't sleep. I've been sitting outside."

"Where outside? I looked outside and I didn't see you anywhere out there."

Maggie sighed. "I went for a walk. Okay? What difference does it make anyway?"

"You've been acting a little strange the past few days. Is there something you want to talk about?"

"You think?"

"What the hell is it, Maggie?"

"That's you in that picture with that woman, Jack. What is she doing with a picture of you?"

"That's not me."

"I know it's you.

"Drop it, Maggie. I'm not having this conversation again."

"Did you have an affair with her, too?"

"You're crazy if you think that."

"I lied to the police for you and they bought it. I guess they figured I'd know my own husband if I saw him. So, how long was it, Jack?"

Jack stared at her for a moment and shook his head. "I'm going to bed."

Maggie glared at him. "Then sleep in the spare room because I'm not sharing a bed with you tonight."

"Fine," he yelled as he walked out of the room.

"Damn right, fine," Maggie shouted back.

"Can you quiet down?" Michael yelled from the top of the stairs. "I'm trying to sleep."

"You woke Mike up. Are you happy now?" Maggie exclaimed.

Jack looked at her, started to say something, shook his head in frustration, and walked away.

"What time is it?" Ida Wickers mumbled.

Chief Wickers looked at the clock that was on his nightstand. "It's three. I've got to go. There's been a fire."

"Be careful," she muttered, as she drifted back to sleep.

Wickers grabbed his cell phone and called Deputy Downing.

"What?" Downing grumbled.

"Wake up. There's a fire out at the nudist camp."

"How bad?"

"I'm not sure. The call just came in. Meet me there."

"I'm on my way," Downing told him, as he jumped out of bed.

"What's going on?"

Downing bent over and kissed Mandy on the cheek. "Go back to sleep," he told her, thankful that she wasn't sleeping at the camp tonight.

Downing pulled in behind the sheriff's car and looked around. He saw Wickers talking to Fire Chief Anders, who was motioning toward the main building, and got out of his car.

137

Wickers turned as Downing approached him. "Nothing to see here, Dan," Wickers told him. "One of the residents put the fire out."

"Where was the fire?" Downing asked.

"Behind the building here. It was set by someone, but they did a piss poor job if they wanted to burn the building down. More smoke than fire."

"What? Someone was just walking around behind the building at this time of night and saw the fire? Don't you think that's a little strange in itself?"

Wickers grinned. "Well, it seems he was anxious to get back to his cabin before his wife woke up."

"I figured that shit went on around here. Do you know who set the fire?"

"No idea. They'll be a full investigation in the morning. Not much we can do in the dark except tape this area off. Rory is here. He can do it. You go on home and get some sleep."

"Thanks, I'm leaving, then," Downing said as he started to walk back to his car.

"Dan?" Wickers called out.

Downing turned and looked at him. "What?"

"Aren't you even going to check to make sure Mandy is okay?"

"What?" Downing replied, looking confused for a moment. "Oh, right. No, I don't want to wake her. I'm sure she's okay or you would have said something. I'll see you in a few hours."

Wickers smiled as Downing drove off.

Jack watched Maggie set the coffee pot down. "We need to talk, Mags."

"I know. I'm sorry I blew up last night. It's just with Alex and everything that's going on – well, I just lost it."

"Maggie, where did you go last night?"

"Really? Do you want to start that again? I told you. I went for a walk."

"Did you hear the fire engines go by?"

"No. When was that?"

"A little before three."

"I was asleep. I didn't hear anything."

"I guess you were tired from your walk," Jack declared.

"What are you getting at, Jack?"

"Someone tried to burn down one of the buildings at the nudist camp."

Maggie stared at him. "You think it was me, don't you? Is that what you're getting at?"

"Was it you? You hate it being there. You wanted it gone."

"For God's sake, Jack, what do you take me for? You think I walked over there and tried to burn that place down?"

"You tell me? It wouldn't be the first time you did something crazy."

"It wasn't me. So, just drop it, will you?"

"I think we should move," he said, looking away.

Maggie didn't say anything.

"It's just a thought. Maybe, after they release Alex's body and we bury him, we can start looking for something else. We don't need anything this big, anyway. I don't know what we were thinking when we bought this." He smiled sadly. "I guess we wanted to give the boys a great place to grow up."

"Well, that's not going to happen now, is it?"

"We still have Mike to think about. This has been pretty hard on him, too, you know."

"I know."

"Will you at least think about it, Maggie? We need to get away from here."

"I can't," she told him, starting to cry. "I can't bury Alex here and just leave him.

"It isn't official that it's him, you know," Jack declared.

"It's him. You know that as well as I do. It's just a formality now.

"Why not have him cremated? We could take him with us."

Jack and Maggie looked over and saw Michael standing in the doorway.

"It's not polite to eavesdrop, Mike," Maggie said.

"I know, but I was only listening for a moment."

"That's not a bad idea, Maggie," Jack declared. "Why not have him cremated?"

"Well, I'm not totally against the idea." She hesitated a moment. "Yes. Let's do that. How do you feel about moving, Mike?"

"The sooner the better."

"And, Mike, not a word about this to anyone," Maggie told him.

He looked at her and smirked. "Who the hell would I tell? I don't know anyone around here."

"Did you get any sleep after you left the camp?" Downing asked Wickers, as he walked into the room.

"A little. I went back to the scene around six-thirty. Anders was already there looking around." He glanced at the clock on the wall. "You certainly slept in. It's almost eleven."

"Sorry. My alarm didn't go off." Downing told him. "Plus, it's my day off."

"Then, what are you doing here?"

"I'm curious. What did Anders say?"

"I don't think we'll ever know who set that fire," Wickers said. "In fact, he isn't even sure it was set on purpose."

"What? Spontaneous combustion?" Downing asked.

"There's a lot of footprints in the back of the lodge along with dozens of cigarette butts. It seems it's a good place to have a cigarette and not be seen. Plus, there is a lot of dried grass and twigs back in that area. He thinks someone probably threw a hot butt on the ground and ignited them."

"Why go back there?"

"Smoking is forbidden at the camp," Wicker said.

"So much for the rules. Besides, where would you carry your cigarettes and lighters?" Downing said, grinning.

Wickers rolled his eyes. "Must be nice to have gotten so much sleep."

Downing shrugged. "It certainly was. Have you heard anything from Doc Dempsey about the Keegan boy?"

"It's Alex. No doubt. The DNA matched. She could determine that he was struck with a heavy object several times."

"Any idea with what?"

"Not yet. She did find a few small splinters of wood. It's being tested to determine where they came from."

"Have you informed the Keegans?" Downing asked.

"I'll drive out later this morning and talk to them. They know it's him, Dan. At least the body can be released now and they can bury their son."

"What do you think happened to him? The only people roaming around in those woods were those two boys."

"And, occasionally Jack and Maggie. Plus, don't forget there are people at both the body farm and the nudist camp. It's not just the family we're looking at here."

"You're right. It could have been anyone in the area."

"Which is why everyone is still a suspect, Dan."

Chapter Twenty-two

"Coffee, Ralph?" Maggie asked Wickers. "I just put a fresh pot on."

"No thanks." He glanced around the kitchen. "Can we sit for a minute?"

"Of course. Jack, do you want coffee?"

"I'll take half a cup," Jack told her. "So, what's up?" he asked, looking at Wickers.

"I'm sure you've already put it together, but I need to officially inform you that the body that was found at the FBI Body Farm has been positively identified as Alex."

Maggie sighed a deep sigh and looked away.

"We figured," Jack commented. "But thanks anyway. Does this mean we can have Alex back now? You know for his funeral?"

"Of course," Wickers replied. "Again, I can't tell you how sorry I am."

"Thank you." Jack reached over and squeezed Maggie's hand. "Are you okay?"

"I'll be fine," she told him.

"Well, I'll leave you to it," Wickers said, standing up.

"Thanks for coming out," Jack said. He glanced over at Maggie and then back at Wickers. "I understand there was a fire at the nudist camp. Do you have any idea what started it?"

Maggie jerked her head up and gave Jack a dirty look.

"We're pretty sure someone threw a lit cigarette butt too close to some twigs and dried-out leaves. We'll never know who it was, of course. One of the members saw it burning before it got out of hand and extinguished it. No big deal."

"To be honest with you, I wish the damned place had burned down," Maggie exclaimed. "Not that I want anyone to get hurt or anything, but I hate that place being there," she added, after seeing the shocked look on Wickers' face."

"That's kind of harsh, Maggie," Jack said.

"Well, I'm sorry. But, that's how I feel. Now if you'll excuse me, I'm going to go lie down. I have a horrible headache."

"She didn't mean that," Jack said after Maggie had left the room. "She's angry at everything and everybody right now."

"No, it's all right," Wickers said. "I guess it's understandable with what you're all going through. Let me know if you need anything, Jack," he said as he opened the front door.

"I will. Thanks again."

Jack hung up the phone and wiped the tears from his face with the back of his hand.

"Is it all taken care of?" Maggie asked, surprising him.

"You scared me. I didn't know you were standing there."

"Sorry. When will it be?"

"Monday."

"Monday? Why so long?"

"The funeral parlor has to pick up the body from the coroner's and prepare ..." Jack shook his head. "I don't know. That does seem like a long time considering that there is nothing to do but cremate him after a private service."

"Call him back, Jack. See if he can have this done by Wednesday."

"That's two days from now. I'm sure if he could do it sooner, he would."

"Would you rather I call him?"

Jack stared at her. "Why don't you do that, Maggie? Why don't you take care of it just like you take care of everything?"

"I didn't set that fire, you know."

"Didn't you?"

"I don't smoke for one thing and if I was going to burn that place down, I'd sure as hell make sure I got the job done right."

Jack took a deep breath and blew it out. "I know. I'm sorry I accused you. How about we get past this and quit fighting? I'm so tired of it all."

Maggie walked over to him and hugged him. "I'm sorry, too. For everything. Let's get Alex taken care of and start looking for a new place to live."

"Where are you going?" Maggie asked Michael as he opened the kitchen door to go outside.

"For a ride. I need some air."

"Absolutely not. I don't want you riding that bike again."

Michael stopped and stared at her. "Just because Alex is dead doesn't mean I have to stop living too, Mom. I've been cooped up here for days. I'm going for a ride."

"I said no."

Michael looked at her, trying to keep control of his temper. "All right," he said after a few moments. "Then, I'm going for a swim if that's all right with you."

"That's fine," Maggie said. "Just be careful."

"Sure thing," Michael replied, as he walked out of the house.

"Where's Michael?" Jack asked.

"In the pool. Would you tell him lunch is about ready?"

Jack glanced out the back door. "He's not in the pool."

"Maybe he came back in. He might be in his room."

Jack walked to the bottom of the stairs and yelled, "Michael, lunch is ready." He waited. "Michael?" he shouted louder this time. "He's not up there," he told Maggie as he walked back to the kitchen.

"Damn him!" Maggie exclaimed.

"What?"

"He's in the woods on that damn bike."

"Are you sure?" Jack asked her.

"Where else would he be? I told him he couldn't use that bike again and he went anyway."

"Do you want me to go find him?" Jack asked.

Maggie thought for a moment. "To heck with him. Let's eat. He'll come back when he gets hungry enough."

Michael parked his bike and walked the rest of the way to the nudist camp, being careful not to be seen. He ducked down low behind a bunch of tall bushes and took out his binoculars. Grinning, he narrowed his eyes in on a red-haired woman who looked about twenty years old.

He was excited to see that she was sunning herself today. He watched as she turned over on her back, exposing the front of her bare body. Feeling himself getting aroused, he pulled down his shorts and started to masturbate.

Suddenly, a man stepped in front of her, blocking his view. "What the ...?" Michael mumbled, as the man sat down alongside the woman and started to caress her breast. Totally erect now, Michael moaned as he blocked out his surroundings and, within seconds, reached satisfaction.

"Do you think he saw us?" the redhead asked the man sitting next to her on the sand.

"I'm quite sure he did," the man replied.

"Good. I figured we might as well give the horny little bastard a show. He just lost his brother, you know."

"I heard," the man said. He rubbed the redhead's stomach, his hand slowly gravitating south.

"What do you think you're doing?" she asked, pushing his hand away.

"I thought maybe we might take our show a little further," he replied smiling.

The redhead grinned and turned over onto her stomach. "The show's done, sweetie, and so are you. Now, go away."

Chapter Twenty-three

"Dan, go pick up Jack Keegan and bring him in."

Deputy Downing gave Wickers a bewildered look. "Why?"

"I need to talk to him and I don't want to do it at his house," Wickers told him.

"So, he's not under arrest for anything?"

"No, I just want to talk to him."

"What if he refuses to come with me?"

"Then convince him that it's in his best interest that I don't have a conversation with him in front of his wife."

Downing shook his head. "Gotcha. I'll go get him."

"Thanks."

"Am I under arrest?" Jack asked Wickers as he walked into the police station. "What the hell is going on?"

"I need to talk to you and I thought it would be better if we did it in private."

"You mean without Maggie."

"That's right."

"Well, there's nothing you can talk to me about that Maggie can't hear. We have no secrets from each other."

"That's good to know. I'll remember that if I need to talk to you again," Wickers told him.

Jack Keegan stared at him, waiting for Wickers to start telling him what this was all about. "Well?" he asked after a few moments.

Wickers looked up from the file he was glancing through and held up a finger. "One minute," he said. He flipped a couple of sheets of paper over. "Ah, here it is."

"What?" Jack asked.

"We ran a DNA test on the fetus from Sophia Regio, Jack. We got a hit."

"Really? What's that got to do with me?" Jack asked, looking away.

"I think you know," Wickers said.

"Tell me."

"It seems that you were the father, Jack. I have to say I find that extremely interesting, seeing as how you claim that you never met the woman."

Jack stared at Wickers for a moment, trying to hold back his anger. "All right. You caught me. So, it was mine. You certainly couldn't expect me to tell you that in front of Maggie."

"I thought you and Maggie didn't have secrets from each other. Or, did I not hear that correctly?"

Jack shrugged. "I didn't kill her. I might have known her but I sure as hell didn't kill her. I didn't even know she was in the area."

"Really? Where did you live before you moved here?"

Jack shook his head no. "I'm not answering that. I haven't done anything wrong and I don't have to answer your questions."

"I'm afraid you do. Unless, of course, you'd like me to charge you with her murder and arrest you right now.

"I had nothing to do with it. I haven't talked to her or seen her in months. Sophia being here in the area and getting herself murdered has nothing to do with me."

"What the hell do you take me for?" Wickers yelled, making Jack jump. "You know as well as I do that she was here to see you. Did she tell you she was pregnant and wanted money? Maybe she threatened that you pay her or she was going to tell Maggie about your affair." Wickers smiled. "But Maggie would have known. Right, Jack? After all, you tell each other everything. No secrets between you two."

Jack shook his head. "You're wrong."

"Am I?"

"One of the reasons we moved here was to get away from Sophia."

"Moved here from where?"

"It doesn't matter from where, Chief Wickers. We won a lottery and we got the hell out of town."

"Did Maggie know about the affair, Jack?"

"Look, I didn't have an affair with her. She was a teacher who seduced a student and got pregnant."

Chief Wickers looked puzzled for a moment. "Are you saying that it was Michael who got her pregnant?"

Jack took a deep breath. "It was such a mess, you know." Jack looked away, obviously upset. "How about that? A kid his age. What the hell was she thinking? Anyway, that was one of the reasons we left Chicago. We didn't know she was pregnant, though. We just needed to get him away from her. The stupid kid thought he was in love with her."

"But we got a DNA match to you."

"I'm his father. Of course, it would be a close match."

"Why didn't you tell me all this when we found her body?"

"And, let you know what had gone on with Mike? We didn't think we'd have to deal with her again. We were as shocked as anyone when her body was found in the lake. We've talked to Michael and he swears he never saw her."

"I'm going to have to talk to him, you know," Wickers told him.

"I imagine you do. He didn't have anything to do with this, though." Jack sighed. "Do you really have to? I don't know how much more of this Maggie can take."

"I'm sorry, Jack."

"Well, let me know when you want to talk to Mike. Do I need to have an attorney present?"

"I can't see that it will come to that," Wickers replied. "By the way, did you press charges against her?"

"No. Maggie just wanted to get away from it all."

"What about the picture? Is that you or not?"

"It's me. It was taken at an open house at the school."

"I wonder why she kept it," Wickers said.

"I can probably answer that."

Wickers glanced at him. "You can?"

"Maggie and I have tried to keep our location secret. However, I figure Sophia must have found out that we moved here. She was probably showing people who live around here the picture to see if they knew me and where we lived. I figure she was going to ask for money."

"Makes sense," Wickers replied.

"I would have paid her if she had asked but I never saw her. Michael didn't do this, Chief Wickers. "He's dumb but he isn't stupid."

"You just told me that he had an affair with his teacher. That's about as stupid as you can get." Wickers

151

stood up and headed for the door. "I'll be right back," He told Jack.

"Where you going?" Jack asked.

"I just thought of something I need to tell Dan. I'll be right back."

"Dan, I want you to go pick up Michael Keegan and bring him in."

"All right."

"Bring him in through the back. I don't want his dad to know he is here. Also, get someone over here from social services. I want an adult here when I question him."

"Will do." Deputy Downing started to walk away, hesitated, and turned back to the Chief. "You got a call from Dr. Dempsey while you were talking to Keegan. I took a message."

"What is it?"

"They found some fibers on Alex's body."

"Did she say from what?"

"She said it looked like it could have come from a beach towel. Also, there was some tissue found under his fingernails. They've run it through the system and haven't found a match."

Chief Wickers looked confused. "Why am I just now getting this information?"

"You'd have to talk to her to be sure, but it sounds like a mix-up in her lab."

"I'll talk to her."

"Okay, I'm out of here," Downing said. "See you later."

"Don't forget, Dan. Bring him in through the back."

"Got it."

152

Chapter Twenty-four

"He's a fucking liar if he said that," Michael screamed at Chief Wickers. "I never did anything to her. She wasn't even my teacher."

"Settle down, Mike. Yelling isn't going to make this situation any better."

Michael glared at him. "Settle down? Fuck that. I'm out of here."

"Sit down, Mike," Wickers demanded, as Michael started to stand up. "We're not through."

Michael stayed sitting in his chair and looked away. "Why would he tell you that?" he said softly, tears filling his eyes.

"As far as I can determine, Mike, is that he was having an affair with her and she got pregnant. He couldn't deny the DNA but he knew it could also point to you. So, he said it was you. Probably so your mom wouldn't know he had an affair."

Michael stared at Wickers as he wiped the tears off his cheeks. He shook his head, not believing what Wickers was telling him. "You're wrong. He wouldn't do that to mom. He loves her."

"How else could that baby have your dad's DNA? Besides, that's why you moved out of Chicago, isn't it? To get you away from her – the woman you think you love."

Michael's head jerked up in surprise. He stared at Wickers for a second and then laughed. "You have to be kidding me. He said I loved her? And, you believe this crap?"

"Why don't you tell me what happened, Mike? Let's get this cleared up once and for all. Did you or did you not have an affair with Sophia Regio?"

Michael sat back in his chair, looked at Wickers, and grinned. "Me screw a woman old enough to be my mother? You have got to be kidding. As God is my witness, I never gave that woman a second look."

"Okay. I'm starting to believe you," Wickers said. "Did your father have an affair with her?"

"Not that I'm aware of," Michael replied.

"Did you know she was in the area?"

Michael shook his head no. "I didn't see her."

"Did you kill Alex?" Chief Wickers inquired.

"What the... Of course, I didn't kill Alex." Michael looked at him. "I'd like a glass of water, please," he said after a few moments.

"In a minute."

"Chief Wickers, the young man has requested something to drink. Would you please provide this for him before you continue your questioning?"

Wickers glanced over at the young social worker and smiled. "Of course. I'll be right back." He stood up and walked out of the room.

Wickers handed Michael the glass of water and sat down at the table. "I'm sorry for my abruptness, Mike, but I've got two murder cases that I'm trying to solve and your family seems to be connected to both of them."

"I loved my brother, Chief Wickers. I would never have hurt him."

"I understand. Do you think anyone in your family hurt him?"

"Of course not," Michael replied. "It's stupid to even think that."

"Why did your family move away from Chicago?"

Michael shrugged. "Mom and dad wanted to move, I guess."

"You guess?"

"Well, yeah. I mean, if they didn't want to move, we'd still be there, wouldn't we?"

"Your dad said it was to get you away from Ms. Regio."

"I already told you that wasn't the reason."

"Did you know that evidence was found on Alex's body?"

Michael didn't say anything.

"We found DNA evidence under his nails."

Michael shook his head, confused. "So, why don't you find out who it belongs to?"

"We're working on it," Wickers replied.

"Well, it isn't mine, as you well know. And it doesn't belong to anyone else in the family. Does it, Chief Wickers? Because if it did, you'd have made an arrest. Besides, I thought we were talking about Sophia Regio, who was a teacher in my old school, who I was not having an affair with, and I'm sick of all of this," he said sarcastically. "Unless you intend to arrest me for something, I'd like to leave."

Wickers sat back in his chair and looked at the young man. "Go home."

As Michael started to stand, Wickers put up his hand. "One thing, Mike."

"What?"

"I want you to think about all of this. Your dad just threw you under the bus and wouldn't you like to know why? I know there's more going on with your family than you want to tell me. I want you to be sure that whatever it is, you're not going to take the rap for it. Because right now it looks like that is what your father is doing. Think about it. He says you got her pregnant, she shows up here, and she's found murdered in a lake where you spend most of your time. I'd say you're looking pretty good as a suspect right now."

"You've got it all wrong," Michael said. He jumped as the door flew open and banged against the wall.

"What the hell do you think you're doing?" Jack Keegan yelled. "How dare you bring Mike here without letting me know first?"

"Sorry, Jack. It's strictly business."

"Come on, Mike, let's get out of here," Jack said.

"Mike can leave," Wickers told Jack. "However, I need to talk to you again. I've got a few questions that need to be answered."

"Are you arresting me?" Jack asked.

"Not at this time."

"Then take your questions and shove them. Next time you talk to me it will be with my attorney present."

"Are you sure, Jack? It would be easier if you talked to me now."

"I'm more than sure. Come on, Mike, let's get out of here."

"Well, if you won't talk to me, I sure hope you will explain to Mike why you blamed him for that baby. I imagine he's got a whole bunch of questions for you."

"Come on, Mike."

"How come you said that baby was mine, Dad?" Mike asked as he stood up and walked towards the door.

"Just shut up, will you? We'll talk about this later."

"But, Dad…"

Jack grabbed his son's arm and pulled him towards the door. "I said later."

"We know that baby was yours, Jack. Why not just admit it?"

Jack turned and stared at him. "No comment." He shoved Michael out the door. "As far as you're concerned, young man…"

"What?" Michael interrupted. "What are you going to do to me?"

"Move it," Jack yelled.

"Jack?" Wickers called out.

"What now?"

"I better not hear that anything has happened to Mike. Understand?"

Jack Keegan turned and glared at Chief Wickers. "I resent that, Wickers. I have never hurt one of my boys."

"That's good to know. Just make sure you don't start now."

Chapter Twenty-five

It was a good ten minutes into the ride home before Michael spoke. "Telling that cop that Sophia was pregnant by me wasn't part of the plan, you know."

Jack glanced over at him and then back at the road. "You should never have talked to him."

"Perhaps you should have told me that you changed the story. A heads up would have been nice."

"I didn't have a chance. I had no idea they were picking you up." Jack glanced at his son again. "I'm sorry."

"So, what now?"

"Let's wait until we get home to talk about this. Your mother needs to be part of the conversation."

"This whole thing is so stupid. Why didn't you just tell the truth to begin with? All that the lying has done is to make you look more suspicious."

"I know."

"Seriously, Dad, this whole thing has gotten out of hand."

"Will you just be quiet," Jack yelled. "You need to shut up for a while."

Michael looked at his father. "You sure have managed to fuck up my life, you know."

"It was already fucked up, Mike. You know that."

Michael slouched down in his seat and looked out of the window. "Mom is going to be so pissed," he muttered.

"You think?" Jack answered.

"What's is going on, Jack?" Maggie exclaimed as Jack and Michael walked through the door. "I've been a basket case waiting for you two to get home."

"Relax, Maggie. Everything is fine," Jack told her.

Michael gave his father a surprised look and then laughed. "You are so full of it," he said. He glanced at his mother. "He's so full of it."

"Let's all sit down, shall we?" Jack asked. "We've got to get this mess straightened out."

"I gather everything is not fine, then," Maggie remarked.

"We need to review, that's all," Jack told her.

"I'm getting a soda," Michael said. "Anyone want anything?"

"Bring me a beer," Jack answered. "Maggie, you want anything?"

"I get the feeling I should have something a little stronger. Am I right, Jack?"

An hour later Maggie finished her drink and sat back in her chair. "So, that's it then?"

"I think so. If Mike can keep his story straight, we should be fine." Jack glanced over at Michael. "Are we good?"

"I'm good. Unless you change everything again and don't tell me," he said sarcastically.

"Don't be a smart ass, Mike."

"I'm good with it," Maggie replied. "I don't like it, but it should work."

"You don't have to like it," Jack told her. "We wouldn't be in this mess if it wasn't for you. There's something else, Maggie."

159

"What's that?"

"It seems that the coroner found some evidence on Alex's body."

"And, we're just now finding out about it? What was it?"

"Fibers for one. They determined that they came from some kind of a towel."

"What else?"

"It seems he scratched someone. They found DNA under his fingernails, but so far no match."

Maggie looked away, tears welling up in her eyes. "My poor baby," she muttered. "Why would anybody hurt him?"

"Are you okay, Mom?" Michael asked as Maggie started to sob.

"She'll be okay, Mike. Why don't you go clean up?"

"You know, Dad, I doubt Alex would have kept quiet if the police had questioned him. He would have spilled the beans for sure. It's probably a good thing he's not around anymore."

Jack hesitated for only a second before he reached out and slapped Michael hard across the face. "Go to your room," he shouted. "How can you even think like that?"

Michael glared at his father as he put his hand to his face. "I didn't mean it like that. I just meant ..."

"I said get out. I don't want to see your face for a while. Understand?"

Maggie stared at Michael, the hurt showing on her face.

"I'm sorry, Mom." Michael turned and walked out of the room.

"Are you okay, Mags?"

"He didn't mean it like it sounded, Jack."

160

"Maybe not."

"You shouldn't have hit him."

"He had it coming."

"I don't think it's a good idea to get him angry, Jack. You should apologize to him."

"No way," he told her, shaking his head no.

"Think about it, will you?"

Jack sighed. "All right. But right now, I'm going for a walk."

Chief Wickers hung up the phone and looked down at his notes. Dr. Dempsey had just relayed the results of the tests that had been run on the evidence found on Alex Keegan's body. Basically, it was what his deputy had already told him. Unknown DNA under the nails and fibers that could have come from a towel. Not much to go on, Wickers thought.

He checked a phone number on his computer, picked up his phone, and called Dr. Simmons at the body farm. He waited. Just as he was about to hang up, he heard a voice say, "Body Farm. How can I help you?"

"Dr. Simmons, please," Wickers replied.

"One moment."

Wickers waited.

"Dr. Simmons here."

"This is Chief Wickers, Dr. Simmons. I wonder if you have a moment to answer a question."

"I do. What can I help you with?"

"Do all of the employees that work at the farm have their DNA on record?"

"May I ask why your need to know this, Chief Wickers?"

"The coroner found DNA evidence on Alex Keegan's body and so far, we haven't found a match in the DNA database. I just wondered if everyone there can be eliminated as a suspect."

"You can eliminate them. All FBI agents' DNA is in the system."

"What about anyone who works there that isn't an FBI agent or trainee?"

"What are you getting at? Oh, you must be referring to Jason Setzman, our handyman."

"That's correct. What about him?"

"It's part of the hiring process, Chief Wickers. You can also eliminate Jason."

"So, everyone who works there has their DNA taken?"

"That's correct."

"Thank you. Sorry to have bothered you," Wickers said.

"No problem. If there is anything else I can do, let me know."

"I will. Thank you." Wickers hung up the phone, sat back, and stared at the ceiling. After a few moments, he yelled for Deputy Dan Downing.

"He's in the john," Officer Canty told him. "He'll be back in a few."

Wickers glanced over at the door as Downing walked into the room.

"I could hear you shouting all the way down the hall," Downing told him. "What's up?"

"Do you still have that list of everyone that was at the nudist camp when Alex Keegan disappeared?"

"Yeah. Why?"

"I want a sample of DNA from every member that was there that day and all of the employees, including Red and Mandy."

"Why Mandy? She didn't do anything."

"Everyone, Dan. Got it?"

"What if the club members that were there that day aren't there now?"

"Then find out where they live and follow up. I want DNA from everyone. And, the sooner the better, so get moving."

Downing glanced over at Officer Canty. "Are you working on anything right now?"

"Nope."

"Then, you're with me. Let's start checking that list."

"Dan, wait a minute," Wickers called out.

Downing turned and looked at him. "What?"

"Do you know if the members bring their towels or if they are provided by the club?"

"I'm not sure but I'll find out. I kinda remember that all the linens and towels are provided seeing as how the club cleans up after the members leave."

"So, the members don't always stay in the same room when they are there?"

"Nope. No one has a set room as far as I know."

"Check that out, too, will ya?" Wickers asked.

Chapter Twenty-six

"Seriously, Dan?"

"I'm sorry, Mandy, but orders are orders."

"Well, if you want my DNA why don't you swab your own mouth? There's plenty of it in there."

Dan grinned. "There might be a little left over from last night," he joked. "Seriously, I need to see your boss and let him know what's going on. Is he in his office?"

"Red is down by the lake working on the boat."

"Is he dressed?"

Mandy smiled. "Red is never dressed."

Robert 'Red' Bean glanced up as Deputy Downing approached him. "Morning, Deputy. You're here bright and early. What can I do for you today?"

"I'm sorry to bother you, Red, but I would like to get DNA samples from all your employees. We're looking for a match to the Keegan boy."

"And, you think one of my employees had something to do with that?"

"Just process of elimination, Red. Do you mind getting them together?"

"I suppose you want mine, too."

"If you don't mind," Downing replied.

"No problem," Red said, standing up and getting out of the boat.

Dan immediately looked away from the man.

Red laughed. "Still embarrassed at the sight of a naked man, are you?"

"Well, to be honest, it's not exactly my favorite thing to look at."

Red laughed again. "Well, come on then. Let's get this over with." He waited as Downing hesitated. "Come on. I won't bite."

"That's everyone who was working here when the boy disappeared," Red told Downing two hours later.

"And, that includes the guests that were here that night," Downing added.

"Right. I'll give the rest a call for you if you want. I'll ask them to submit to a DNA test and to get back to you to set it up. How does that sound?"

"That's great, Red. Thanks for your help. I appreciate it and I know Chief Wickers will also. I'll be in touch."

"Look forward to it. I wonder if you'd like to spend a few days here as my guest. You know, get used to being one with nature."

"I'm not sure I'm ready for that," Downing replied grinning.

"Think about it. You know the old saying – don't knock it until you try it."

"Oh, one more thing," Downing said. "God, I almost forgot."

"What's that?"

"Your towels. Do you provide the towels for your members or do they bring their own?"

"What in the world does that have to do with the Keegan boy?"

"Do you provide them?"

"Well, yes. We have fresh towels in the rooms and cabins, but a lot of our members bring their own beach towels. They are a lot larger than what we provide and they take them down to the beach. I guess I'd say they use ours for showering and stuff and their own for the beach. Does that help?"

"Kinda. Where do you buy your towels? Do you always buy the same kind?"

"We usually get the same make of towel."

"Could I borrow one?" Downing asked.

Red looked at him, obviously confused. "You want one of our towels?"

"If you don't mind."

"Deputy, I'm not sure exactly what is going on, but I can tell you right now that no one from this camp hurt that boy."

"And, you're probably right, Red. I doubt we are going to find anything here that connects to his death." Downing hesitated a moment. "I probably shouldn't tell you this, but some fibers were found on Alex's body. They most likely came from a towel. We need to check your towels to see if there is a match."

Red shook his head. "You're really reaching, aren't you? You need a towel? Take your pick. I guarantee you're not going to find a match. Hell – take 'em all. You're still not going to find a match. This is the dumbest thing I've heard and I've heard some dumb things in my life."

"Perhaps it is. But we have a dead boy and we'd like to find out who killed him."

"I get it. But – well, do what you need to do. What about the woman from the lake? Have you figured out who she was yet?"

"We have a name. It's still an open investigation."

"You sure have your hands full, don't you? Well, let's get some of those towels for you." He yelled for Mandy, who was in the reception area.

"Is that enough?" Red asked fifteen minutes later. Downing glanced down at the pile of towels and grinned. "I think these will do just fine," he replied.

"We aim to please," Red told him smiling.

"I'll get these back to you as soon as possible," Downing told him.

"No need. Plenty more where those came from." He glanced at Mandy. "Thanks."

"My pleasure, Red," she replied. "Anything else?"

"That should do it. Right, Mr. Deputy?"

"That should be it. Thanks for your time. It's appreciated."

Downing hesitated as Red stood up and reached out to shake his hand. After a moment, he took Red's hand and shook it. "Thanks, again."

Red grinned. "Better check that hand, boy, and make sure there aren't any cooties on it."

"I'll walk you out," Mandy told Downing.

Red sat back in his chair and watched Downing and Mandy walk out of his office. He sighed as he stared at Mandy's ass. "Damn, that's nice," he muttered.

Deputy Downing walked straight to Wickers' desk and deposited the towels. Wickers looked at Downing and frowned. "You didn't need to bring all of these," he told Downing.

"I know, but Red volunteered so I took them. I also have DNA samples from everyone that works at the camp

167

and from the guests that were staying there when Alex was murdered."

"Anybody give you a problem about it?"

"Not a soul. Everyone was more than happy to help out. Even the members that weren't even there that day wanted to give a sample. Plus, Red is contacting the rest of the guests that were there that day and asking them to come in so we can take a sample."

"Good. Let's get the lab on these right away." He glanced up at Downing. "What?"

"Nothing. It's just that I've never seen so many people willing to cooperate."

"Maybe naked is better," Wickers replied, grinning.

Chapter Twenty-seven

"It's been two days," Deputy Downing remarked. "Shouldn't we have heard something by now?"

Chief Wickers glanced up from his desk and shook his head. "We can't rush these things, Dan. You know it takes time."

"I'm dating Mandy from the Nature Club," Downing blurted out, looking uncomfortable.

Wickers sat back in his chair and stared at him. "And, you're telling me this why?"

"Because I don't want to go behind your back any longer. I thought you should know."

"I thought we talked about this, Dan. She's on the suspect list."

"That's nuts. We both know she had nothing to do with either of those killings. The DNA will prove that."

Wickers sighed. "I was hoping you'd keep this under wraps until after the investigation was over."

"You know?" Downing asked, looking surprised.

Wickers chuckled. "What do you take me for? I'm a cop. Of course, I know. I just didn't want to *know*, if you get my drift."

"Well, then, forget I said anything."

"I don't know if I can do that. The cat's out of the bag now."

"What cat? I have no idea what you're talking about." Downing looked away, smiling.

"Perhaps you best put the cat back into the bag, Dan. And, keep her there until this investigation is over."

"You mean don't see her?"

"For a while. Can you do that?"

Downing thought for a moment. "I'll try."

"Don't try, Dan. Do. Okay?"

"Okay, Chief. I'm sorry about this. But she is so frickin' hot. Man, when I see her, I just want to..."

"What? Dress her?" Wickers said grinning.

Downing laughed. "She isn't always naked, you know."

"Don't you have work to do?"

"Yes, Sir. Sorry I bothered you."

"How was lunch?" Downing asked his boss as Wickers walked into the room.

"It was okay. Any news?" Wickers asked.

"You had a call from the forensics lab that has been going over Sophia Regio's car. It looks like they've found something. An Agent Bacbuster wants you to call him."

"Number?"

"On your desk."

Downing watched Wickers make notes as he spoke to Agent Bacbuster on the phone. He figured it was good news when he saw Wickers smile, write something down, thank the agent, and hang up.

Wickers looked at Downing and grinned.

"Something good?" Downing asked him.

"Could be," Wickers replied. "They've traced prints that were found in the car back to Jack and Maggie Keegan."

"You're kidding?"

"Nope. And, that's not all. There was a towel found in the trunk."

"Do you think that's where the fibers on Alex's body came from?" Downing said, looking confused. "Wait. Sophia was found before Alex disappeared. So, what would a towel have to do with her? Any fibers from that towel wouldn't match the ones found on Alex. Timing isn't right."

"You're right. The timing isn't right for Alex, but Michael Keegan's DNA was on the towel.

Downing's mouth dropped open at the news. "No way!" he exclaimed. "You're telling me that all three of the Keegans were in that car?"

"Well," Chief Wickers replied, "at least two of them were and the DNA match from Michael Keegan came from his sperm."

"So, he did have sex with Sophia Regio."

"Well, he either used that towel to wipe off after he masturbated or wiped off after sex. Or, she used it to wipe off, but it's there."

Downing grinned. "Looks like you got the little bastard. What now?"

"Now, Dan, I'm going to make a little surprise visit to the Keegans."

"Can I come with?"

"First I want you to get an arrest warrant and a search warrant from the judge."

"Whose name on the arrest warrant?"

Chief Wickers looked at him and then shook his head. "I'm not really sure." He thought for a moment. "All of them. We'll figure it out as we go along."

"Nobody's home," Downing said. "We have the search warrant. Do you want to break the door in?"

"Why don't you check the back door first? Maybe it's unlocked." Wickers turned and motioned for the rest of the officers to go round to the back of the house.

Wickers stood on the porch waiting for his officers to check the back door. Suddenly, the front door swung open.

"Come on in," Downing said. "The back door wasn't locked.

Wickers walked into the living room and looked around. "All right, guys, you know what to do. I want every room in this house gone through with a fine-tooth comb. Find me something."

"What about the computers?" Officer Canty asked.

"We'll take those with us and have the computer geeks check them out," Wickers replied. "Okay, men, move it."

"Nothing. Absolutely nothing. I can't frickin' believe it," Wickers exclaimed angrily. "There has to be something. Where the hell are they hiding it?"

"Maybe, there isn't anything to find," Downing said.

"Oh, there's something, all right." He walked over to a small table and picked up a coffee pot.

"Maybe, the computer guys will find something," Downing commented.

"Let's hope. Who has eyes on the house?" Wickers asked as he poured himself a cup of coffee.

"Canty and Tash. They're on until midnight. Hopefully, the Keegans will be back before that."

Wickers glanced at his watch. "I'm leaving for a while. It's Ida's birthday and I promised to take her to dinner. Call me if there's any news."

"Where are you going to eat?"

"Mitchell's"

"Wow! You're going big tonight."

"Ida deserves the best. I'll see you in a few hours."

"Give her my best," Downing called out as Wickers walked out of the room. "And, wish her a happy birthday for me."

Jack Keegan pulled the Lincoln over to the side of the road and put the car into park. "Do they seriously think we can't see them parked there?"

"Do you think they saw us?" Michael asked.

"I don't think so. They are facing the other direction."

"Let's go home, Jack. So what if they are waiting for us? They can't do anything."

"I'm not in the mood to deal with cops tonight, Maggie. The Sullivans are gone for a few days. How about we park behind their house and walk home through the woods."

"Sounds good to me," Maggie told him.

Jack backed the car up a few feet and turned into the Sullivans' driveway. He carefully made his way around the house and parked in their backyard. "I don't think you can see the car from here," he commented. "Let's go."

Chapter Twenty-eight

"Turn that light off," Keegan yelled.

"Sorry," Michael said.

Maggie walked into the living room and looked around. The light from a full moon was shining through the windows, making it just bright enough to see without turning on any lights. "Either we've been robbed or the cops have been here."

"Are you sure?" Jack asked as he walked into the room.

"Things have been moved."

"My computer is missing," Michael yelled from upstairs. "It looks like someone has gone through all my stuff."

"Check the den, Jack, and see if our computer is gone, too."

"It's gone," Jack called out a moment later.

Maggie plopped down on the couch and yawned. "I'm beat. I'm going to bed."

"How can you even think about sleeping with the cops outside?" Jack inquired.

"Because they have no idea that we are here."

"Was there anything on our computer to be concerned about?" Jack asked.

"Of course not. Unless you been looking at kiddy porn, that is."

"It looks like they've skipped out," Deputy Downing declared.

"If they did, they didn't take anything with them," Wickers said. "It didn't look like anything was missing when we searched the house yesterday."

"What are we gonna do?"

"I think we should watch the house a little longer. The problem is, Dan, they have more money than God. They could take off and leave everything and just buy more stuff. Let's put an APB out on the car and see if we get a hit. They are out there somewhere and I want them found."

"Chief, phone call," Officer Canty called across the room.

"Take a message," Wickers told him.

"It's Jack Keegan," Canty said.

"Well, why didn't you say so in the first place." Wickers picked up the phone. "Jack, good to hear from you."

"What the hell is going on, Chief? We go for a ride and come home to find that our house has been broken into."

"We had a search warrant, Jack."

"Oh, I found your warrant. Tucked away in the dining room under the floral arrangement. We found it this morning."

"I need to talk to you, Jack. Mike and Maggie, too. Do you want to come in or should I send a squad around to pick you up?"

"We'll come to you, Jack. Let me call my attorney and I'll get back to you with a time."

"Make it soon, Jack. We've got a lot to talk about and I'd rather you come in on your own."

"I'll call you back."

"Wait a minute."

175

"What?"

What time did you get home this morning?"

Jack laughed. "Your men need a little training on surveillance, Chief. We've been home all night. Bye."

Wickers stared at the dead phone. "Son of a bitch," he exclaimed.

"What?" Downing asked.

"He said that they've been home all night."

"No way," Downing declared. "He's pulling your leg. Our men would have seen him."

"Obviously not. Is Tash still out there?"

"Yeah. You want me to tell him to come on in?"

"No, I want you to tell him to give me a call as soon as the Keegans leave the house."

Jack hung up the phone and let out a deep sigh. "Nelson is sending a local attorney over to sit in with our interviews."

"He's not coming?" Maggie asked.

"If he has to. He said he's going to wait and see what's going on before he makes the trip. In the meantime, we'll have to settle for the local guy. I'll call Wickers and let him know we're on our way and to watch for the attorney."

"Ready, Mike?" Maggie asked her son.

"Let's just go and get this b.s. over with."

"I want you to be on your best behavior, Mike. Understand?"

"Yes, Mother, I understand," he replied sarcastically.

"Want some fun?" Jack asked, trying to lighten the mood.

176

"I could use a laugh," Maggie replied. "What?"

"How about I go get the Lincoln and pick you up? That will blow that cop's mind."

"This isn't funny, Jack. Let's just take the Highlander and go. You can pick up the Lincoln later."

"I'm getting it. You and Mike wait here. I won't be long."

Maggie watched as Jack walked out the back door and ran into the woods. She looked at Michael and smiled. "Are you okay?"

Michael glanced up at her and shook his head no. "Of course, I'm not okay. The cops want to talk to me about that woman and you and dad keep changing stories. Just trying to keep everything straight is giving me a headache. Everything is so messed up, Mom."

"I know and I'm sorry, Mike. But, let's just play this smart today, and pretty soon we'll be able to put all this behind us."

"God, I wish we'd never moved here," Michael cried out.

"I know, sweetie. Me, too."

Fifteen minutes later, Officer Tash, picked up the radio and called Wickers.

"What's up?" Wickers asked. "Have they left?"

"Well, something weird is going on. Keegan just pulled into his driveway, the wife and kid came out of the house and got in the car, and they all drove off. He's headed towards town."

"Say again, Tash."

"The wife and kid were home but Keegan just got there. He picked up his family and I figure they are on their way to the station."

"That doesn't make sense. He said he was home when I talked to him. What kind of a game is he playing, anyway?" He hesitated a moment. "Follow him, Tash. Make sure he isn't headed someplace else. And, let me know if anything changes."

"Will do. I could pull him over and arrest him if you want."

"No. Just make sure he shows up here."

"Ten-four. Over and out," Tash said and broke the connection with his boss.

Chapter Twenty-nine

"Can I get you something? Coffee? Water?" Wickers asked Jack.

"Let's get this over with, shall we?"

Wickers sat down at the small table, reached over, and flipped a switch on a tape recorder next to him. "It is 10:45 am on August 23, 2020. This is Chief Wickers, investigating officer interviewing Jack Keegan. Also present are Officer Dan Downing, Mr. Keegan's attorney Mr..." He glanced at the gentleman sitting next to Jack Keegan. "Would you state your name for the record, please?"

"Harry Winston, attorney for the Keegan family."

"Thank you. Harry Winston is also present." Wickers looked down at the file in front of him and shuffled some papers around. "Ah, here it is." He read through the paper and put it back on the table. "Jack, I'd like to know where you were last night."

"I already told you. I was home."

"I see. Were Maggie and Michael also at home last night?"

Jack grinned. "We were all home last night, Chief. Why? What happened last night?"

"I'd like an explanation why your fingerprints were found in Sophia Regio's car."

The grin disappeared as Jack's head jerked up and he stared at Wickers. "They what?"

"You heard me. Your fingerprints were in her car. I'd like to know why."

"That's impossible." He looked at the attorney sitting next to him. "He's lying, Harry."

"I'd advise you to not answer that question," Winston told him.

"No comment, but I know you're trying to trick me up, Wickers. I was never in her car."

Wickers smiled. "How about an explanation why Maggie's fingerprints were there, too? What do you have to say about that?"

Jack glared at him. "No comment."

"Well, maybe Maggie will tell me when I talk to her."

"She won't say diddledee because you're lying."

"Okay, Jack. Here's what I think. I think Sophia came to your house looking for money. She's pregnant, will probably lose her job if she hasn't already, and you tell her that you need to go to the bank first. You tell her to meet you out on Old Quarry Road and you'll give her the money. You meet her, you get in the front seat with her, and Maggie gets in the back seat. Suddenly Maggie wraps a rope around her neck and strangles her. Sophia fought, though, didn't she, Jack? I imagine you held her down while Maggie finished her off. Or, was it the other way around? Perhaps Maggie was in the front seat and you were in the back. Doesn't matter, though, does it? You're both going down for her murder."

Jack started to object when his lawyer shook his head no.

"No comment," Jack told Wickers.

"Then, you put her in the trunk of your car, drive her home with you, and in the dark and quiet of the night you carry her through the woods, and toss her in the lake like a bag of garbage."

"You're crazy if you think…" Jack quit talking and looked away. "You're crazy if you think I killed her."

"Well, I don't think Maggie could have done this all by herself, Jack, and both of your prints were all over her car."

"No comment."

"We're also going through both of your vehicles as we speak. I imagine we'll find Sophia's DNA somewhere in one of them. Most likely the trunk. Or did you just leave her lifeless body in the front seat with you while you drove home?"

Jack took a deep breath and let it out. "No comment."

"Of course, there's another scenario that could have happened. But I'll talk to Mike about that one."

"You keep Mike out of this. He didn't have anything to do with this," Jack yelled.

"Oh! Well, all right, then. So, it was just you and Maggie then. Is that what you're telling me?"

Jack sat back in his chair and stared at Wickers. "No comment, you prick."

"Prick? Really, Jack, I thought you were above name-calling. So, here's your chance to come clean and tell me what happened. We know you knew Sophia and we know you had an affair with her. We know she was trying to blackmail you about the baby – your baby. And, we know you killed her. Would you like to add anything?"

"No comment."

"Mr. Winston, I'm going to go talk to Mrs. Keegan. Would you like to accompany me?"

"Yes."

"Interview suspended at 11:52 am." Wickers reached over and flipped a switch, turning off the recorder.

"Would you care for something to drink?" Wickers asked the attorney as they stood outside the interview room

"Do you have any coffee?" Winston asked him.

"We do. I figure I could use a cup myself." He glanced over at Officer Canty, who was watching them. "Two coffees, please, Rory. Do you use anything?" he asked Winston.

"Black is fine."

"Make those both black, would you, Rory?"

"Sure thing, Chief," Canty responded.

"Are you up for this, Harry?" he asked the attorney.

"For now. I plan on calling Nelson as soon as we're done here. This is more his bag than mine. But I figure I can at least advise them for now."

"It's gonna get worse. You sure you don't want to call him now?"

Harry Winston studied the Chief's face for a moment. "That bad, huh?"

"Yep. You might want to make that call."

Harry Winston and Chief Wickers placed their coffee down on the table and sat down. "How you doing, Maggie?" Wickers asked.

Maggie didn't reply.

Wickers reached over and turned on a recorder, went through the introductions of the people in the room, and sat back in his chair. "You're in trouble, Maggie. Big trouble. So, instead of me going through what I know, how about you tell me what happened to Sophia Regio? And, don't leave anything out. Okay?"

"I have no idea what you're talking about," Maggie said softly.

Wickers sighed. "All right. Let me try again. We found your fingerprints in her car. We know you were there and that you killed her. Jack says he only helped get rid of her body."

Maggie grinned. "I'm sure Jack said all that. You're a horrible liar, Chief."

"We still haven't found what you used to strangle her. Tell me, was it a rope or what?"

Maggie mimicked a fisherman throwing out a line. "Do you fish a lot, Chief?" she asked.

"I'm waiting to hear from the forensics lab. They are going through your cars as we speak. I'm quite sure we're gonna find Sophia's DNA in one of those cars. Aren't we, Maggie?"

Maggie stared at him, not answering him.

"Wait a minute. I think I have this wrong. Mike was there, too. Wasn't he? You and Jack caught him with Sophia. That's why you killed her. Of course. Now it all makes sense. Sophia picked Mike up and they drove out to Old Quarry Road. You and Jack followed and found them together. Were they making love, Maggie? Did it make you so angry you killed her? Of course, that's why there was a towel found in her car with Mike's DNA on it. Did you know that? His DNA – his sperm."

"You leave Mike out of this. You hear me?"

"I can't leave him out of it. His DNA proves he was there. It proves he had been with her, Maggie. I guess he's going down with the two of you. One of you killed her and the other two helped cover it up. I've got you."

"You have shit!" Maggie cried out. "You have nothing!"

"Interview suspended at 12:15 pm." Wickers reach over and turned off the recorder.

Harry Winston followed Wickers out of the room. "Are you questioning Michael Keegan next?"

"I am."

"Give me a minute, will you? I'm going to give Nelson a call."

Chapter Thirty

"Remember, Chief, he's only a kid. You'll need to tread lightly," Harry Winston said.

"That's why you're here," Wickers replied, as he opened the door and they entered the room.

Michael jumped as the door opened. His left leg was shaking and he looked terrified.

"Michael, would you like some soda or something?"

Michael glanced up at him. "I'd like to use the washroom."

"No problem. Just out the door to your left. What kind of drink do you want? Coke or Pepsi? I think we might have 7-Up also."

Michael stood up. "Coke is fine."

Ten minutes later, Michael walked back into the room and sat down. He looked at a can of 7-Up on the table in front of him. "I wanted Coke."

"We were out. This will have to do," Wickers told him, glancing at the can of soda.

Michael picked up his soda and took a swallow. "Thanks."

"I'm recording this, Michael, if that's okay with you."

"Fine."

Wickers turned on the recorder and went through the procedure. "Okay, now I'm only going to ask you a couple of questions, Mike. There's no reason to be nervous. I've already talked to both of your parents and I just need you to confirm a few things that they told me. Okay?"

Michael shook his head yes.

"Out loud, please. For the recorder," Wickers said.

"Sorry. Yes."

"Good. Now, this first question might be a little embarrassing to answer so let's get it out of the way. Okay?"

"Okay."

"Did you at any time have sex with Sophia Regio? Either when you were living in another city or here?"

Michael's face turned red as he shook his head no.

"Out loud, please."

"No. I never had sex with her."

"Are you sure, Mike?"

"Of course, I'm sure."

"Could you explain why we found a towel in the trunk of her car with your DNA on it?"

Michael looked surprised. "No way. I was never near her car."

"So, you don't know why a towel with your sperm on it was found in her car?"

"Well, I sure as hell didn't put it there. Someone else must have put it there."

"Why would someone do that?"

"I have no idea," Michael replied shrugging.

"Your mom told me that she and your dad caught you with Sophia having sex in her car, Michael. She said you used the towel to wipe off."

Michael looked confused. He glanced over at Harry Winston. "What do I say?"

"I think you should probably not say anything, Michael. No comment is probably best."

186

"No comment," Michael told Chief Winston.

"All right. Let's get back to that. Did you know that Sophia was in the area?"

Michael looked away, not answering.

"Mike, did you?"

"I was pretty sure I saw her but I figured it couldn't be her, seeing as how she was so far away from where she lived. Then, a few days later, I saw her car drive by the house again. Alex can tell you. He was…" Michael bit his lower lip. "Sorry, sometimes I forget he's gone."

"It's okay. So, you're saying that both of you saw her drive by your house."

"Right."

"Did you tell your dad about it? That you had seen her?"

"Alex did. He told dad that we thought it was a teacher we knew. Dad just laughed it off and told us to forget it."

Wickers made a few notes on the pad in front of him. "How could anyone have a towel with your sperm on it, Mike?"

Michael shook his head. "I don't know. I mean, I guess mom could have taken it out of the wash. Sometimes, I…"

"That's okay, Mike. I get it."

"But that doesn't make sense. Why would my mom put a towel in the trunk of Ms. Regio's car?"

"Think about it, Mike. We know that it wasn't your baby she was pregnant with. Tests proved that, but your dad blamed it on you. Now, it looks like your mom planted false evidence against you."

"But, why?" Michael asked looking confused.

"I think they killed her and are trying to set you up to take the blame."

Michael closed his eyes, thinking about what Wickers had just told him.

"Are you okay, Mike?"

"Have you found out who killed my brother yet?" Michael asked.

Wickers stared at him. "Why?" he asked after a few seconds.

"Just wondering."

"Michael, if you know something about Alex's death you have to tell me."

"I don't know for sure."

"Tell me and I'll check it out."

"Maybe you should check out the towels at our house."

"But we already know that the towel found in Sophia's trunk was from your house."

"What about the fibers on Alex's body? What if those are a match?"

"I would expect them to match, Mike."

Michael looked away. "I guess. Forget I said anything about Alex. But I never did anything to hurt Ms. Regio and I never screwed her. My parents are big fat liars."

"I should let you know, Mike, that we're planning on arresting your parents for Ms. Regio's murder."

"Go ahead. It won't stick."

"What do you mean, it won't stick? What aren't you telling me, Mike?"

"No comment. Can I go home now?"

"Are you planning to arrest Michael, Chief Wickers?" Harry Winston asked.

"Not at this time."

"Are you planning on arresting his parents at this time?"

"They will be detained, yes."

"Then, I'm requesting that you allow Michael to leave with me. I've already discussed the different scenarios of what could happen with Jack. He asked me to take guardianship over Mike if he and his wife were arrested. At least until Mr. Nelson arrives. Mr. Nelson will then be staying with Mike at his house until this mess is figured out."

"I'm not sure if I can agree to that."

"Broderick Nelson is close to the Keegans. They've been good friends since before Michael was born. Nelson is more than capable to take care of him."

"I was not aware that they had such a close relationship," Wickers told him. "All right. I'll agree to this arrangement for the next forty-eight hours. We'll see after that."

"Thank you, Chief Wickers." Winston turned to Michael. "Come on, Mike. How about we get something to eat and after I'll take you home with me?"

"Can we go to my house first? I have to feed the dog."

"Well, let's go get him. He can stay with us for now. What's his name?"

"Beast. Alex named him."

Winston glanced over at Wickers, who was grinning.

"Good luck," Wickers said.

Chapter Thirty-one

"I'm Broderick Nelson. I understand you are holding Jack and Maggie Keegan here."

Officer Rory Canty glanced up from his desk. "Are you their attorney?" he asked.

"That's right. I'd like to speak to my clients."

"Have a seat over there. I'll be right back," Canty told Nelson.

Nelson turned and studied the chair that Canty had indicated. "It's dirty. I'm certainly not sitting on that."

Canty shrugged. "Suit yourself." He got up from behind his desk and walked over to Chief Wickers, who was speaking on the phone. Wickers glanced at him; a questioning look on his face. "The Keegans' attorney is here," Canty told him.

Wickers looked over towards the door and saw Nelson standing by Canty's desk staring at him. "Hold on a moment," Wickers told the person he was talking to. "Is that Nelson?" he asked softly.

"Sure is," Canty told him, holding back a grin. "He wants to see his clients. Should I take him back to an interview room to wait?"

Wickers studied Nelson for a moment. "How much do you figure he weighs?"

"How should I know? Maybe three-fifty or four hundred."

"I don't think we have a chair big enough to hold him," Wickers said.

"There's that bench down in the locker room. How about Tash and I go get it and put it in the interview room?"

"You do that. I'll keep Nelson occupied."

Officer Canty motioned to Officer Tash to join him and they hurried out of the room. Wickers stood up and walked over to Nelson. He held out his hand, "Mr. Nelson, I'm Chief Wickers. Good to meet you."

Nelson shook hands with Wickers. "Same here." He looked around the room. "I'd like to speak to Jack and Maggie."

"We're bringing them up now. It will just be a minute or two. How was your drive?"

"I flew in this morning. Don't drive if I can help it."

"How did you get here from the airport?"

"I rented a car. I have my driver with me."

"I see. Can I get you some coffee?"

"No, thank you. This is all a big mistake, you know. Jack and Maggie did nothing wrong."

"Well, I guess that's for the courts to decide. We have a great deal of evidence against them, Mr. Nelson."

"And, I'll bet you a dollar that it's all circumstantial."

Wickers looked over and saw Canty motioning to him. "You need something, Officer?"

"Room is ready, Chief. Officer Tash is bringing the Keegans up now."

"Thanks. Mr. Nelson, if you'd like to come with me, I'll show you to the interview room you'll be using."

Nelson followed Wickers down a short hallway to the room. "How much time do I have?" Nelson asked, glancing at his watch.

191

"As much as you want. There's a buzzer by the door. Ring it if you want anything or if one of you needs to use the restroom. Just wait for an officer and let him know what you need."

"Thank you." Nelson walked into the room, noticed the bench by the table, and sat down. "Thank you," he said again. "You're very considerate."

Wickers closed the door and walked back to his desk.

"How did he seem?" Officer Canty asked.

"Nice enough."

"Did the bench break?" Canty asked grinning.

"Be nice, Rory."

"Well, a fine mess you've got yourselves in," Nelson commented as Jack and Maggie sat down at the table.

"It's gotten totally out of hand," Jack told him. "If that damn teacher hadn't shown up, none of this would have happened."

"Your prints were all over her car, Jack. Are you saying they just magically appeared there?"

Jack shrugged. "So, we were in her car. However, that was in Chicago. Not here. "

"What about Mike? Is he involved in this in any way whatsoever?"

"Absolutely not," Maggie exclaimed.

"What are they saying about Alex? Any suspects there?"

"The cops don't have a clue," Jack replied. "Look, Alex dying was an accident."

Nelson stood up and stretched. "Who did it?"

Maggie and Jack looked at each other. "We'd rather not say," Jack told him.

Nelson started pacing the floor. "Let me think a minute about this." He glanced over at the buzzer. "I want something to drink. What about you guys?"

"I could use some coffee," Maggie replied.

"Me, too. And make it a large one," Jack told him.

Three hours later, Broderick Nelson opened the door and walked out of the interview room. He walked down the short hall and looked into the room where Wickers was sitting. "Chief, a word, please," he called out.

Wickers looked over at him and smiled. "Certainly. What can I do for you?"

"Are Jack and Maggie eligible for bail? What's the deal here with that?"

"I'm formally charging them today. They've been here almost forty-eight hours and I need to act or let them go. I'll be asking for them to be remanded until trial. No bail."

"You'll only need to charge Maggie. She has admitted to killing Sophia Regio."

Wickers looked at him, shocked by his news. "Are you telling me that Maggie has admitted to this?"

"I am. And, she acted alone."

"There's no way she could have killed Sophia, carried her body to the lake, and dumped her in. She had to have some help."

"She swears she acted alone. Jack did not participate in any way."

"What about Michael? Did he help her?"

"That's not up for discussion. Maggie will tell you everything, but only if you promise to leave Jack and Mike out of it."

"I don't know if I can do that," Wickers told him.

"Isn't a bird in the hand worth more than two in the bush, Chief Wickers? Her confession will clear this case for you. And, it will also clear up Alex's death."

Wickers stared at him. "She killed her son?" he exclaimed.

"She didn't kill him. Alex's death was an accident, but she did hide his body."

"Why didn't she tell us if it was an accident? I don't believe this."

"It will all come out when she talks to you."

"Actually, she needs to speak to the District Attorney. I'll give him a call."

"Tell him that she wants a guarantee of immunity for both Jack and Michael."

"I thought they were innocent," Wickers said sarcastically.

"They are. This will guarantee that they will not be prosecuted at any time now or in the future if some DA decides to pull a fast one."

"I'll tell him when I call. I'm not sure if he'll go along with it, though."

"It's either that or nothing," Nelson told him.

Wickers glanced at his watch. "I'm going to arrest Jack and Maggie first. Would you like to accompany me?"

"Jack, too?"

"For now. I can always un-arrest him later."

Chapter Thirty-two

"The District Attorney is here," Officer Downing told Wickers.

Wickers waved at a nicely dressed man standing in the doorway and motioned to him to come over to his desk. He stood up and shook the man's hand. "Good to see you again, Paul."

"You, too. Are you sure about this, Ralph? It seems a little fishy to me."

"She's confessed to killing the Regio woman and hiding her son's body after he died. We've got her on both counts. There won't be a trial, which will save the taxpayers a lot of money. I'm good with it. Did you bring the letters of immunity with you?"

"I did. Is their attorney here? What's his name again?"

"Broderick Nelson," Wickers told him.

"*The* Broderick Nelson? From Chicago?"

"You know him?"

"Not personally. Man, the name didn't ring a bell until now. I didn't realize their attorney was from out of state. For your information, Broderick Nelson is one of the best criminal attorneys in the country. He's represented some of the worst crooks all over the United States. How the hell did the Keegans get him?"

"I understand he's a good friend of theirs. Their friendship goes back years."

"How the hell can they even afford him?" Paul asked. "Or, is he doing this as a favor?

"Oh, I'm sure he'll get paid. The Keegans won a big ass lottery a while back. Millions of dollars."

"Some people do have all the luck, don't they?" Well, shall we get started?"

"Everyone's in a room just down the hall. Would you care for a cup of coffee?"

"So, I guess that takes care of that," Wickers commented an hour later. "I gather everyone is satisfied."

"I am very satisfied," Broderick Nelson replied. "Jack, that's it for you. Stick around and we'll pick up Mike and go for dinner."

"You and your driver can stay with me for a few days," Jack told him.

"I planned to," Nelson replied. "Maggie, I'll talk to you later."

"I'll be driving her over to the county courthouse tomorrow morning," Wickers said. "After today, you'll need to talk to her there."

"Of course," Nelson agreed.

Jack took Maggie's hand and held it. "Are you going to be okay?"

Maggie smiled and squeezed his hand. "Of course. You just take good care of Mike. You hear me?"

"May I kiss Maggie goodbye?" he asked Wickers.

"Of course." Wickers stood up. "How about we give them a few minutes to themselves?"

"You know what to do?" Maggie asked Jack.

"Of course. Nelson and I will pick up Mike and take him home. We'll wait there until they arrive."

"Nelson said it wouldn't be until tomorrow morning sometime. You sure you'll be okay?"

"What could happen? Mike and I have immunity, so we're good."

"Broderick did a good job, didn't he?" Maggie asked.

Jack grinned. "He always does a good job. That's why he makes the big bucks."

"I wonder what this is gonna cost us," Maggie said.

"Who cares. Whatever it is, it's worth it."

"I guess you should go."

"I know. Don't worry, Maggie. We've got our go-bags ready. Is there anything in the house that you want to bring along?"

"No, but what about Beast?"

"Beast is part of the family. He'll come with us."

Jack took Maggie in his arms and hugged her. "I love you."

"I know."

"I'm so sorry about that Sophia thing. I seriously thought we were far enough away that she'd never find us."

"Shit happens, Jack. And, remember, she seduced Mike. It wasn't his fault."

Jack sighed. "I know."

Maggie pulled away and looked into Jack's eyes. "See you soon," she said.

"Not if I see you first," he replied, smiling.

At nine-thirty the following morning, a black SUV with darkened windows pulled into the Keegans' driveway. Two men dressed in black suits and wearing dark sunglasses exited the vehicle and entered the house.

Five minutes later, the two men accompanied by Jack Keegan, Michael Keegan, and a little Yorkshire terrier named Beast, exited the house, got into the SUV, and drove away.

At nine-thirty-four, three FBI agents dressed in black suits and wearing dark sunglasses walked into Chief Wicker's police station and flashed their badges.

"What can I do for you?" Wicker's asked as he stood up, feeling slightly intimidated.

"We are here to pick up Maggie Keegan," one of the men told him.

"I'm sorry, but Maggie Keegan is under arrest. I was just getting ready to drive her to the county courthouse for her arraignment."

"Sorry, but that's not going to happen, Chief Wickers. We have instructions to pick her up. Mrs. Keegan is in the Witness Protection Program. Her cover has been compromised and we will be relocating her and her family."

Wickers plopped back down in his chair and stared at the man. "She what?" he finally asked.

"I don't believe I need to repeat myself." He turned and looked at his accomplices. "Give Chief Wickers the papers, please."

Wickers stared at the papers for a second and threw them on his desk. "This is bull shit," he exclaimed. "She killed someone."

"That might be, but we are taking Mrs. Keegan with us. Would you please make her available? Now."

Wickers glanced over at Office Downing, who looked shocked. "Chief, can they do that?"

"Go get her, Officer Downing."

"No way. She killed that woman. They can't just take her and let her get away with murder."

Wickers looked away.

Downing stared at Wickers, disbelief written on his face. "Can they?"

Chapter Thirty-three

Two miles out of Prairieville, SD, the two black SUVs pulled over to the side of the road. Jack and Mike got out of the first vehicle and walked to the car behind them. Jack opened the door and they got into the back seat.

"Did everything go okay?" Jack asked Maggie.

"It was a breeze," she told him.

"How you doing, buddy?" Jack inquired, smiling at Mike.

Mike glared at him. "How do you think I'm doing? I'm sick of this crap. Let's just go."

Jack settled into his seat and sighed. "You may be sick of this crap, Mike, but it's still better than jail."

"Whatever. And, you can stop calling me Mike now. My name is Cody, in case you've forgotten."

Jack took Maggie's hand and grinned. "Janice."

Maggie smiled and squeezed his hand. "Clark, good to see you again."

The driver turned and looked at his three passengers in the back seat. "Buckle up, people. It's going to be a long ride." He held out his hand. "Phones."

"Really?" Cody whined.

"You know the procedure, son. Hand it over."

"Where the hell are we?" Clark asked, looking out the blackened window of the SUV. The vehicle had stopped in the driveway of a modest-looking home. He rolled down the window, surprised that it was light outside. "How long have I been asleep?"

"This is it. Your new home," the agent said, ignoring Clark's questions.

"It's about time," Janice commented, yawning. "Where are we?"

"You're at 2300 Dana Lane in Kalispell, Montana."

"Montana? My god, if you keep moving us, we'll end up in the Pacific Ocean."

The house is unlocked. You can go in," the agent told them.

"Aren't you coming in with us?" Clark asked.

"No need. The refrigerator is stocked with enough food for a week. There is a car in the garage for your use. You'll find your clothes in your rooms. All the documents you need are on the kitchen table – birth certificates, social security cards, driver's licenses – well, you know the routine."

"I think we'll have to buy a different house," Janice said. "I mean, this is a real comedown after what we had."

"I don't think that will be possible, ma'am."

"Why not?" Clark asked.

"The people who oversee the Witness Protection Program will be handling your money from now on. You will get an allowance each month that will be enough to live on. You'll need to get jobs if you want additional spending money."

"What the hell are you talking about?" Clark yelled. "That's our money. You can't do that."

"I'm sorry, but we can and we did. You'll find everything you need in these packets. Agent Bridwell?"

The man in the passenger seat turned and handed three large envelopes with names written on the front to

Clark. "One for each of you. Read and learn. This is who you are now."

"Clark, what's going on?" Janice asked, obviously distressed by the situation.

"It looks like things have changed a little," he told her. "Excuse me, Agent, but could I make one call before you leave with our phones."

"To who?"

"I'd like to talk to my attorney, Broderick Nelson, and find out what's going on. We didn't agree to this."

"Sorry, no. You have new phones in the house with new numbers. You should know that your calls will be monitored. We will know if you violate the rules again."

Janice opened the car door and got out. "Come on, guys. Let's go check out our new dump."

"What's my new name?" Cody asked as he got out of the SUV.

Janice walked into the house and looked around. "My God, I'm back in the fifties."

"So, we'll fix it up a little. And, please don't start complaining about everything. We're stuck here, so let's just make the best of it."

"Marion?" Cody yelled. "They named me Marion! Do they think I'm a girl? No way! I'm not using that name. No way!"

Clark grinned. "It could be worse. They could have called you Digby."

"Not funny, Dad."

"Did you know that Marion was John Wayne's real name?

Cody stared at him. "So?"

"If it was good enough for him, it's good enough for you."

"God, you're such an idiot," Cody exclaimed.

"Watch your mouth," Clark yelled.

"That's enough, you two," Janice stated loudly "Here, take him, will you?" she asked handing the little dog to Cody. "He needs to be walked."

"Why do I have to do it?"

"Because I said so."

Agent Bridwell glanced over at his partner and grinned. "Well, they weren't happy campers, were they?"

"True. But it will only be for a little while."

"Why do you think we had to bring them so far this time?"

"They really screwed up. You know, getting away with one murder is par for the course in this business. But, two? Plus, this isn't the first time."

"When should I hit it?" Bridwell asked.

"Let's wait until we're out of town. We intersect with Hwy. 2 about a mile or so from here. We can take that right into Seattle, where we'll catch our plane."

Janice plopped down in an overstuffed chair and sighed. "This place is crap. I'm not going to like it here, Clark."

"Well, you better get used to it, because ..." Clark hesitated.

"Because what?"

Suddenly and without warning an explosion rocked the neighborhood, destroying the modest little home at 2300 Dana Lane, instantly killing Maggie and Jack.

Michael woke up a few feet from the tall fence that surrounded the backyard. He slowly raised his face out of the dirt and turned his head, looking at the rubble where a house had sat only seconds ago. He glanced to his right and called to his little dog. It only took a moment to realize that Beast was dead, having been impaled by a huge kitchen knife that was sticking out of his chest.

Michael's ears were ringing and his body ached from head to toe. He pushed himself into a sitting position and took a deep breath. "Those sons of a bitches tried to kill me," he stammered.

He stood up and looked around, still feeling wobbly from the explosion which had thrown him across the backyard. He took a few deep breaths, felt his head start to clear, and the ringing in his ears slightly diminish.

"Shit!" he exclaimed, hearing sirens wailing in the distance. Not wanting to be seen, he grabbed the top of the fence and pulled himself up. Throwing a leg over the top, he managed to drop to the other side of the fence. He was on a vacant lot.

Michael brushed his hair back off his face and straightened out his clothes. Hearing the sirens, which sounded closer now, he started walking in the opposite direction of the noise, hoping he was heading toward town.

Michael sat as far back in the bus as possible. He laid his head back, closed his eyes, and wished his heart would stop racing. He smiled when he felt the bus finally move.

"Okay, everyone. Sit back and get comfortable," the bus driver announced over his intercom. "It's a long way to Chicago."

THE TWISTED TREE TRIANGLE   Susan L. Paré

About the Author

I was born in Idaho in 1939. My father's job demanded that we frequently move and, by the age of ten, I had lived in Idaho, Montana, Colorado, Michigan, and Wisconsin. By the time I was eight, I knew the names of every tree in the woods and was proficient in reading a map. No GPS back in those days.

Dad finally quit moving us from town to town and in 1949 we settled down in a small town in Wisconsin called Columbus.

Eventually, I married and had three sons. I have two fantastic grandsons and, as of today, two great-grandchildren on the way – one a boy and one a girl – both due in July 2021. I have no plans to acquire another husband, as they are just too much work.

In 2014, I wrote my first book, *Blueberries and Bears and My Brother's Shoes*, a book about growing up in the forties and fifties. After I self-published it and gave it to friends and family to read, they encouraged me to get serious about my writing.

I never thought that, at the age of 76, I would become an author. I enjoy the sense of accomplishment and I set a goal for myself to write at least ten books before I die. Now six years later, I've just finished number seventeen. Fortunately for me, the stories keep coming.

I enjoy a good laugh and figure it's my sense of humor that keeps me going when times are tough. Reading has always been one of my passions and I still read a couple of books a week.

I certainly am enjoying my retirement knowing, when I get up each morning, I have something to look forward to. Check out my books and me at www.susanlpare.com. Please visit me there, sign up to be on my readers' list, and feel free to send me your comments.

Susan L. Paré

www.ingramcontent.com/pod-product-compliance
Lightning Source LLC
Chambersburg PA
CBHW071906220626
47052CB00002B/232